OPEN ARMS

THE SABELA SERIES - BOOK 7

TINA HOGAN GRANT

REVIEWS

"Open Arms is a must read! You will laugh, cry, and want to keep reading." - *Karen Wright*

"The author exposes the dark side of life striking a chord of injustice and desire for the reader to reach out to protect the characters. Ms. Hogan Grant continues to add intriguing twists to keep her plot lines credible. I highly recommend this five-star novel." - *Author - Ashley Cobb Post*

"I have truly enjoyed reading the entire Sabela Series and Open Arms is no exception. Tina Hogan Grant knows how to connect with readers through her wonderful writing and the right emotions that touch one's heart." - *Reena Argwal Gilja*

"I absolutely loved this book. This book took us thru Travis and Clare story. Without any spoilers I would say I couldn't put the book down. I can't wait for the final book in the series. The author didn't disappoint. Definitely read the series." - *Robin Rennert*

CHAPTER 1

Claire

This wasn't just a honeymoon for me, it was also much-needed alone time with Travis, and a chance to wrap my head around what had happened at our wedding. I've been numb ever since the horrific incident and couldn't talk about it to anyone, not even Travis. He's tried to talk to me and console me, but I've been pushing him away, remaining silent, and letting him know I can't talk about it yet, I'm just not ready.

To avoid thinking about it, I've been keeping myself busy spending time with Travis' mom Caroline, getting to know her better, and working diligently with Travis at the Children's home which we've named *Open Arms*. Our hard work has finally paid off, and we'll be officially taking our first group of children in after returning from our honeymoon camping vacation near Yosemite.

I still can't believe this is happening! It's been a dream of ours and we've worked so hard to make it come true. It's definitely brought us closer together. Through all of the difficulties, as well as spending so much time working together, I've realized we make a good team. It didn't go so well in the beginning, Travis recovering from his accident and suffering fatigue and mood swings. But as his health improved so did his attitude, and working with him has been wonderful. I know *Open Arms* will be a tremendous success.

Since our wedding and the death of my brother Davin, the days have been okay as I've not allowed myself to think about it, but the nights, not so much. It's been almost two weeks since that dreadful evening at our wedding reception and I've woken up every night in a sweat; screaming and reliving the death of Davin, and hearing the gunshot when Davin shot Slater just before my brother died.

I've tried to stay up as late as possible because I don't want to close my eyes. When I do I fear the nightmares will return. I've tried falling asleep in Travis' arms, feeling his embrace and scent, hoping that feeling the security of his arms around me would fend off the terrible dreams, but so far it hasn't.

Travis begged me to talk about it, but I just can't; just where would I begin? I tell myself I'm happy Davin is dead, but am I? And then there's my anger when I think of my parents. I trusted them, and they broke that trust with their lies and the way they deceived me. Their actions crushed me - I don't know if I can ever trust them again.

I picked up my phone from the nightstand next to my bed where I'd been lying for the past hour, checking the time. Travis had left an hour ago to get ice for the ice chest and get gas. As soon as we load everything in the truck we'll be getting on our way, beginning the road trip for our honeymoon. We have no reservations, just a plan to wing it and set up camp when happen upon a place that appeals to us.

It was already 8:00 AM and Travis wanted to be on the road no later than 10:00. I shook my head and tried to pull myself out of the depressed state I found myself in.

I'm about to leave on my honeymoon with the man of my dreams and I refuse to let the ghosts from our wedding destroy it, I told myself. I managed a slight chuckle when I heard Tilly bark with joy from the living room when Caroline, Travis' mom, asked her if she wanted to go outside.

After I heard the front door close which told me I was alone in the condo, I pulled myself out of bed and hopped into the shower before packing the last of my toiletries for the trip.

When Travis returned, I was sitting on the edge of the bed putting on my jeans. He entered the room wearing a huge smile, and came and sat next to me, lifting my spirits immediately. I loved him so much, and knew that when I was ready to talk, he would be there for me, just like he'd always been.

He wrapped his arm around my shoulder and pulled me in. "Hey wifey." That was my new nickname since our wedding. "We have a full tank of gas and ice in the ice chest. I'm going to load up the truck. Are those all the bags by the door?"

I nodded while I stood and buttoned my jeans. "Yep, that's it, and all the camping gear is in the spare room."

Travis stood and faced me, resting his hands on my shoulders. "You had another nightmare last night. Are you okay?"

"Yeah, I'm good. I'm sure when I'm snuggled up to you in a tent under the stars, I won't be having any bad dreams."

Travis squeezed me and gave me a long, drawn-out kiss. "That's my girl. Come on, let's get out of here. You're the only person I want to spend time with for the next week."

CHAPTER 2

Travis

I'm worried about Claire. She's good at putting on a front and pretending everything is okay, but I know her well and she's hurting. Her eyes don't lie, they are the windows to her soul, and I see only sadness which is tearing at my heart.

I don't want to pressure her to talk to me for fear I may push her away, but from experience, I know it's the only way she will heal. She needs to let me in before the loss of her brother and the severed relationship with her parents destroy her. I refuse to just sit back and watch the woman I love bear so much pain and heartache and try to handle it alone. I'm here for her and always will be, just like she was there for me after my accident.

I grabbed two of the bags by the bedroom door and left Claire to finish dressing when I saw my mom and Tilly at the front door. Tilly raced through the condo after her morning stroll, barking at our bedroom door until Claire let her in.

"Hey mom, did you have a pleasant walk?" I asked.

My mom looked at me with love flowing from her eyes, which

I never tire of looking at. I've only known her for ten days, but I feel like I've known her all my life. Thanks to Claire and Jill, I got the best wedding present I could ever dream of when they found my mom and invited her to our wedding, which is where we met for the first time.

Over the years, since first finding out I was a foster child, I'd often wondered what my mom was like. My whole life I'd felt like an outcast with no sense of belonging. Thanks to my amazing wife, I no longer feel that way, and my mom's feeling of guilt which has haunted her most of her life for giving up her only child are subsiding, replaced with happiness after us being reunited.

We're still getting to know each other and have thirty years of catching up to do, but we're off to a good start. It can only get better from here since she's accepted our invitation to be the nurse at *Open Arms* and live with us full time instead of returning to her life alone in Seattle, where she'd been a nurse for several years.

I am so proud of her and know that I get some of my strengths from her. After allowing her life to spiral out of control after giving me up, turning to drugs and alcohol for escape, but then successfully turned her life around and got her nursing degree. Now she'll be able to help other children in need at *Open Arms* with her skills.

My mom turned her head from where she was fixing Tilly's food. "Yes, it was a wonderful walk. What time are you leaving?

"As soon as we've loaded the truck; I'm going to take these bags out and come back for more."

My mom nodded. "Do you need a hand?"

"No, you just watch Tilly, make sure she doesn't escape," I laughed.

After giving Tilly her food, my mom followed me to the door and opened it. "Thanks," I said, heading down the hallway to the elevator.

When I returned for more, I found Claire in the spare room putting more bags by the front door.

"Hey, how are you doing?"

She looked up and gave me a weak smile. "I'm okay. I can't wait until we're on the road." She pointed to the things by the door, "those are ready to go."

I stood before her and gave her a caring smile, placing my hand on her shoulder. "We're going to have a fun time, okay? This'll be good for you. It'll be just you and me for an entire week."

She smiled. "I know, I love you so much."

"And I love you."

I stood up and grabbed some more stuff. Claire quickly followed with her arms filled. "I'll help you," she said, following me out of the room.

After we loaded everything in the truck, including the ice chest full of food and drinks, we joined my mom in the living room where she sat with Tilly on the couch watching TV.

"Okay mom, we're ready to go. You're in charge now, and you have Slater and Sabela's numbers, right?"

"Yes, you texted them to me and they're on my phone. Will you have cell phone service where you're going?"

"I'm not sure, but just in case we don't I wanted you to have their numbers. We'll try to call you every day, but not to worry if we don't, it's most likely because we have no service."

My mom waved her hands, "Tilly and I will be fine, don't you worry. Now go have a nice time and I'll see you next week."

Claire leaned in and hugged my mom. "Thank you so much, for everything."

"Oh, you don't need to thank me Claire, after what you've done for me it's the least I can do. It's been a long time since I've been able to call anyone family," she smiled. "That's what you and Travis are, family."

I hugged my mom. "Yes, we are mom, we love you."

We were on the road by 9:30, with me doing the first part of the driving while Claire studied a map on her phone of our route.

"If we take Interstate 5, then the 99, then hop on to the 41, it's

400 miles," she said, glancing at her phone. "Once we're out of LA we can find a place to eat. What do you think?"

"Sounds good to me. Hey, do you want to check out Sequoia National Park? Depending on what time we get there, we can probably find a place to set up camp or get a motel room."

Claire's eyes lit up, which made me smile. "Yes! I was there many years ago." Her smile quickly disappeared before she continued, "with my parents and Davin, we were just kids. He was a normal kid back then. I think I was around ten, maybe eleven, and Davin must have been in his teens."

It was the first time Claire had mentioned Davin as a childhood memory. I kept driving, looking straight ahead, hoping she'd say more, but she only had two more words.

"Damn him," she hissed, flopping back in her seat.

I decided not to pursue it or pressure her with questions. This was a delicate and emotional time for her. I needed to allow her to release any thoughts at her own pace so she could hopefully move forward. Just the fact that she'd mentioned Davin within the first ten minutes of our trip was a good sign. I had a good feeling about this trip, my gut was telling me Claire would return home in a much better state of mind than where she is now, it was my turn to save her.

CHAPTER 3

Claire

I'm shocked by how just the mention of the Sequoias ignited a childhood memory of Davin I hadn't thought about in years. I had to silence myself to push back the tears I knew would explode if I continued thinking about it. At one time in our lives, we were normal kids - brother and sister. We were close, he was my big brother who looked out for me and protected me; when did all that change? When did Davin change?

I shook my head to erase the memories, turning to Travis and giving him a forced smile. "Let me know when you want me to drive."

"I will, you just lay back and enjoy the scenery."

I chuckled. "I will when we get out of the city. Not much to see here from the freeway but a bunch of concrete."

After passing through Bakersfield, we took a detour towards the Sequoias and stopped in the quaint town of Three Rivers. As we parked in front of the restaurant I stepped out of the truck, stretching my arms and breathing in the fresh air. "Wow, it's beautiful out here! What a beautiful place to live, look at these cute little cabins right on the river."

Travis approached me and wrapped me in his arms. "Yeah, you really feel like you're living when you stand amidst nature and the great outdoors, we need to do this more often."

I patted his chest and looked up into his eyes with my arms around his waist. "It's going to be hard to get away once *Open Arms* is officially open for business."

"Well, we'll just have to bring all the kids with us, it'd be good for them."

I smiled. "I love it, nothing better than seeing children enjoying Mother Nature, what a brilliant idea. We'll make plans for some trips with the kids." I pulled away, releasing a nervous laugh. "Listen to me, I'm talking like a mother."

Travis quickly moved his hands to my shoulders and gave my body a gentle shake. "That's because you'll be their mom, and from the way you're talking about our future kids, you'll be a natural."

I blushed at the thought as a gush of warmth raced through me. "Yeah, you're right. They'll be our kids. I guess it's slowly sinking in Travis, we're going to be parents."

Travis took me in his arms, embracing me and giving me a tender kiss on the lips. "That's right, in less than a month we'll have a family."

We both turned and looked at the restaurant as the sweet aroma of burgers and fries seeped from the building. "Come on let's get something to eat, I'm famished," Travis said, taking my hand.

We ate outside on the deck facing the river, the cool breeze and fresh mountain air were too good to pass up. I looked across at a table where a family of four sat. The high-pitched squeals from the two young girls caught my attention when a grey, bushy tailed squirrel scurried across the top of the wooden railing next to their table. Laughter soon broke out amongst the family once the little visitor left.

I stared at the beautiful family making memories. The girls were adorable dressed in their hiking boots, jeans and T-shirts, backpacks lying next to them. I envisioned Travis and I making memories here with our kids.

I smiled at what I'd just seen. "Did you see that? What a wonderful experience for those kids, so much better than Disneyland."

Travis nodded and smiled at the family as the mother, seemingly in her late thirties with short blonde hair looked our way. "Are you guys camping out here?" Travis asked.

"Yes, we bring the girls here every year, they love it. Chloe is ten, and this is her fifth time here and Lindsey is eight."

I smiled at the two girls. "That's wonderful, what a great family vacation."

Travis finished chewing his burger before he spoke. "Can I ask where you're staying? We just got here and plan to visit the Sequoia National Park tomorrow."

The woman's eyes lit up, "oh, you'll love it, we were there yesterday. We go every time we're here." She turned to her husband, "what's the name of the campground we're staying at?"

Her husband leaned forward past his wife, "we're at the Kaweah Oaks Campground, right on the river."

"Do you know if they have any vacancies?" he asked, tapping his phone.

"I'm not sure, we always book months ahead of time," he replied.

Travis looked up from his phone. "Thanks, I found the website, I'll check it out. Enjoy your vacation."

"What a nice family, we're definitely bringing the kids here." I waited a few minutes asTravis continued to browse on his phone. "Any luck?"

"Maybe, it looks like they have a spot open. How lucky is that? Give me a sec, I'm going to see if I can reserve it."

"Really? Wow, we got lucky."

After a few minutes, Travis laid down his phone and leaned back in his chair. "All set, we got the last spot at the campsite, they must've had a cancellation or something."

After finishing our meal and saying goodbye to the nice family we headed straight to the campground to set up camp before dark. We worked on the tent together, and after the chairs and ice chest were in place, we headed down to the river which was less than a minute away.

I immediately kicked off my sandals and sat on the bank, placing my feet in the chilly water. "Oh, this is heaven." I patted the ground, "come sit next to me and get your feet wet," I told Travis who was standing behind me.

Travis wasted no time and was soon sitting next to me, his feet dangling in the water. With his arms wrapped around my waist, we watched two teenage girls float by in black inner tubes. "That looks like fun," I said, waving and smiling at the girls.

"Yeah, if it was earlier in the day, I'd find a place where we could rent or buy a couple so that we could've spent the afternoon on the river," Travis said, waving at the girls.

I leaned into Travis, nuzzling my head against his chest. "This is just perfect for me, sitting here in the shade with the sound of the river flowing by on this beautiful warm night. Soon the sun will set and we'll be able to see the stars," I said raising my head to gaze into his eyes. "This is all I want, just you, me and nature."

Travis kissed the top of my head. "It's what I want too, wifey. You've made me the happiest man in the world."

I pressed my head firmly against his chest and breathed in his scent. Suddenly images of Davin as a young boy swimming in a river somewhere haunted me; I quickly pushed them aside and squeezed Travis' hand, "you make me happy, too."

Travis

We remained on the banks of the river for a few hours. Claire sat between my legs, her arms resting on my knees and my arms wrapped around her shoulders. We sat still saying few words. Just being with each other in solitude and nature was heavenly. Once the sun went down and the skies turned black, we found ourselves mesmerized by the hundreds of stars twinkling in the sky.

Claire leaned back and rested her head against my chest as she looked up and said, "Wow! Imagine seeing that every day! Another reason I wanted to spend our honeymoon camping and not in some hotel!"

"It sure takes your breath away, I feel like it's just you and me, and that we're on another planet."

Claire released a heavy sigh. "Yeah, it doesn't get any better than this does it?" Suddenly she sat up and pointed up in the sky. "Did you see that? It was a shooting star; I've never seen one before!"

I stared hard at where she was pointing, "I don't see it."

"It's gone now, but wow, that was amazing!" She patted my knee, "keep looking, there'll be another along."

"Did you make a wish?" I asked.

She turned her head and gazed into my eyes. "I did, but it's already coming true, I'm spending my days with the love of my life."

For the next few minutes our eyes were fixed on the sparkling stars, then we both jolted up at the same time, "I just saw one," I yelled the same time Claire did. "There's one!" Claire squealed.

"Wow! That was awesome!" I said, eyes wide. "That's the first time I've ever seen one, too."

Claire turned her head and smiled, "this is so romantic."

I leaned in and gave her a passionate kiss on the lips. "You know what would make it even more romantic?"

Claire grinned, "no, what?"

"Holding you close to me, both of us naked in our double sleeping bag."

Claire rubbed my thighs, then turned around and knelt before me. I leaned in to kiss her again.

"I like that idea," she whispered. "It's getting a little chilly out here, are you ready to go now?"

I took her hand. "No time like the present."

We didn't have a large tent. It was barely big enough for two people, and if we bent our heads down, we could stand up looking at the ground. I crawled into the tent first and quickly undressed before sliding my body into the sleeping bag. Claire waited at the opening of the tent until she saw she would have enough room to undress.

From under the covers of the sleeping bag, my hands resting behind my head, I watched with bated breath as Claire slowly undressed before me. Man, she was gorgeous, my manhood stirring as I watched her take off her pants and T-shirt. She smiled and flirted as she peeled off her underwear and unsnapped her bra, tossing it onto my face. I laughed and held it up and took in her scent. I detected a trace of perfume in the silky material. Claire turned to close the opening of the tent, then paused as she gazed outside. "I can see the stars from here, do you mind if I leave it open?"

I looked through the opening from where I lay. "That's a gorgeous view; yes, leave it open."

Claire smiled and crawled into the sleeping bag next to me. Her body was chilly against my warm skin, and I gasped as her thigh touched mine. "Oh, you're cold. Come here and let me warm you up," I said, rubbing her arms.

I pulled her into my arms, rubbing her chilled shoulders which were still exposed to the chilly air swirling around inside the tent. Embracing her in my arms, we both rested our heads against each other and looked out through the opening of the tent. There was a slight breeze and the branches on the trees ruffled like stirred feathers. I could hear only a few voices from a campground further down.

Claire released a heavy sigh of pure bliss. "Can you see the stars?"

"I can, this is heaven."

"Shh, do you hear that?" she whispered, "I think it's an owl."

I held my breath as my ears perked up, and soon heard the distant sound of an owl. "Yes, I hear it," I whispered.

Claire reached over and hugged my upper torso. "I never want to leave this place, I love you so much, Travis."

I leaned in and cradled her chin with my hand before kissing her on the lips. "I love you too," I said, my chest heaving from the scent of her hair blanketing my face. We continued to kiss passionately as we pressed our naked bodies hard against each other beneath the sleeping bag.

I reached down and circled her waist with my arms, pulling her on top of me, her breasts resting firmly against my chest. She smiled and kissed me again, "it feels so good to be your wife, Mrs. Claire Kent," she said with an enormous grin.

I chuckled and squeezed her waist. "No, it's wifey."

Claire rolled her eyes and giggled. "Wifey sounds good too," she said, pressing her lips against mine.

"Hmm, you taste and smell so good," I whispered, stroking her thigh and squeezing her butt cheeks. "Your skin's so soft. I want to make love to you beneath the stars."

Claire responded with a shift of her body, lowering her head onto my chest, coating it with light kisses and soft strokes of her tongue. I moaned from the touch of her lips on my bare skin, raking my hands through her hair as she worked her way down to my stirring manhood.

After caressing my now prominent erection with her sensual mouth and tongue, I knew I wouldn't be able to hold back much longer. I tugged at her hair, "I want you," I gasped, my chest heaving.

Claire looked up and smiled before positioning herself again on top of me, slowly easing down onto my erection.

We both released a loud, satisfying moan as I entered her, and then we became one. We rocked slowly, holding her hips as we made beautiful love in the cozy tent beneath the stars, the light wind of the cool breeze funneling into the tent.

After we both had climaxed, Claire remained on top of me, panting, as I held her in my arms. Sweat beaded up on our foreheads and bodies, moist beneath the hot sleeping bag.

"I'm so hot," Claire said between heavy breaths, struggling to roll off my chest and unzip the double sleeping bag. After a few minutes, she hastily pulled up the top part of the bag and flopped her body down next to mine.

"Oh, that cool air feels great. Do you mind if we leave the tent open all night? I just love hearing the wind travel through the trees and the sound of the water flowing in the river."

"I love that idea. Now let's try to get some sleep so we can get an early start in the morning."

CHAPTER 5

Claire

After packing up our tent we headed back into the cute town of Three Rivers to stop for breakfast at the same restaurant where we'd met the nice family the day before.

It was only 7:30 in the morning but the place was bustling with hikers, families and locals eager to start their day with new adventures.

After a hearty omelet breakfast, we headed up the windy road which had breathtaking views on our way to Sequoia National Park. We made it to the park before 9:30. After we parked I stepped out and gasped at the giant redwoods surrounding us. The site was breathtaking and mind-boggling at the same time.

"Wow, look at the size of these trees, they're amazing," I said, as I stood in awe.

Travis took off his baseball cap and tilted back his head. "Wow, they're incredible. I wonder how old these trees are?"

"Some are 1,000s of years old - in fact, I read somewhere that this park is the home of the oldest living Giant Redwood named General Sherman. We should look for it, they say it's over 2,000 years old."

Travis' jaw dropped. "Wow! That's incredible!"

I strained my neck to look up at the wonders of the amazing forest. I felt so tiny amongst the giants, they must be over 200 feet tall.

Travis looked up, taking in the beautiful scenery which surrounded us. "They're magnificent, I've never seen such a sight."

We stood wrapped in each other's arms for a few moments, mesmerized where we stood. Across from where we parked tourists stood in front of the gift shop taking pictures of historical monuments, and up ahead of us on the road, cars were stopped, and a crowd of people were standing on the road.

"I wonder what's going on over there?" I said, staring at the crowd.

Travis took my hand. "Let's find out. Come on, let's put some drinks and snacks in a backpack and check it out before we go for a hike. I want to see as much as we can before we head out this afternoon."

I closed my eyes and breathed in the fresh scent of the trees again. "Sounds good."

Travis carried the backpack and after locking up the truck we headed over to the crowd of people. As we drew closer, I noticed many were off to the side of the road taking pictures, while others were shushing the crowd to be quiet.

"There must be something over there," I whispered as we made our way to the front of the crowd - then we saw the spectacular sight, crossing the road was a mama bear and three cubs.

I took Travis' hand and gasped, "oh my god, will you look at that!" I whispered.

We both froze as the crowd allowed the beauty of nature to bless them with their presence, mama bear boldly leading her family across the road before us.

"She's so big," Travis whispered, his eyes wide.

"Yeah, you don't want to come between mama bear and her cubs. Wow, they're so cute," I said, quickly snapping a few pictures with my phone.

We continued to watch as the bears made it to the other side of the road and up the embankment into the forest.

"That was amazing, another first for me," I said with a huge smile.

"Me, too." Travis glanced around and pointed to our right. "That looks like a trail over there."

We left the crowd which was now standing around in groups looking at their pictures on their phones, then headed for the trail.

It was a narrow dirt trail surrounded by Giant Redwoods, and we could hear the trickle of a small creek off in the distance. After walking across the small wooden bridge over the creek, the trail led us to an open space of even grander redwoods with enormous trunks.

"Wow, check these trees out," I gasped, heading over to a plaque to read about the history of the Giant Redwoods.

Travis stood behind me and wrapped his arms around my waist, resting his chin on my shoulder as we read the plaque together, learning the history of the Giant Redwoods and the park.

We spent the next hour walking the trails through the forest of magnificent trees in awe of their beauty until I came to a sudden stop near a huge rock where a few children were laughing and shouting as they climbed to the top of it. But it wasn't them I saw; it was Davin and me, we were kids playing on that rock. I held my hand up to my mouth, tears pooling in my eyes. "Oh my god, I remember it like it was yesterday." I remained still, unable to move. A daunting chill swept through my body.

Travis turned and faced me, "remember what?" he asked with a creased brow.

I continued to stare at the rock. "I played on that rock with Davin, he helped me to the top, he was always looking out for me."

I fell to my knees, my hands raised against my face as I cried. After suppressing my emotions over Davin's death they'd finally surfaced, and there was nothing I could do to hold them back. "I lost my big brother, and it hurts," I cried.

CHAPTER 6

Claire

Every bone in my body turned to rubber, and I trembled from the overwhelming grief which suddenly consumed me. Travis knelt beside me, cradling me in his arms as I collapsed onto the ground and buried my head in his chest. I couldn't stop the gush of tears or the wails of pain as Travis rocked me in his arms.

"It's okay, let it out," he whispered, as hikers stared and walked around us.

I tried to sniff back my tears, but they wouldn't stop. I cried louder, trying to block Davin's voice in my head. "Come on Claire, I'll help you climb to the top, just take my hand, I know you can do it."

"I can't Davin, I'm scared," I'd said.

Davin had continued to hold out his hand and I looked into his eyes and trusted him. "I trusted you, Davin!" I screamed from Travis' arms.

Travis continued to rock me. "There you go, just let it out Claire, let it go."

My eyes were closed, and all I saw were Davin's blue eyes, then I heard him again. "Come on, Claire. I won't let anything happen to you."

"You promise Davin?" I'd said from the base of the rock as I slowly held out my trembling hand.

"I promise, sis, I would never let anything happen to you."

"You promise you won't let me go or leave me if I climb to the top?"

Davin took my hand, "I would never leave you, sis."

I cried louder and squeezed Travis' arm. "You lied Davin! You said you'd never leave me!" I opened my eyes and stared at the large rock which had triggered the memories from my childhood. I tried to wipe away my tears, but they were instantly replaced with fresh ones. Still wrapped in Travis' arms, his sleeve drenched from my tears, I heard my parents' voices, both cheering me on to climb the rock. "Go on, Claire, you can do it, Davin'll help you," my dad hollered from nearby.

It drew me back to that day, and I remembered everything so clearly, just as if it was yesterday. A memory I didn't know existed or thought important enough to remember. I stared at the top of the rock. Davin had my hand; we were halfway up. He never let go and continued encouraging me to climb. I held his hand tightly, digging my nails into his skin as we triumphantly reached the top, and as I stood next to Davin holding his hand and feeling so proud, I looked down at my parents and waved "look! I made it, I got to the top!" I hollered.

My tears softened and I pulled away from Travis' hold, pulling myself up. Travis stood with me, remaining silent as I walked towards the rock and began climbing. It seemed a lot smaller now than when I was a little girl and I made it to the top in no time. A slight breeze tickled the back of my neck as I spun my head, and whispered, "Davin, was that you?"

I glanced around the top of the rock, folding my arms and lowering my body into a sitting position, my knees up high at my chest. What happened to you, Davin? I didn't lose you the night of our wedding, I lost you long before.

Travis climbed onto the rock and took a seat next to me. "Hey, mind if I join you?"

I gave him a weak smile, "I'm sorry, this silly rock took me back to my childhood when Davin helped me climb it." Tears pooled in my eyes again. "When he was a young boy, he was a good brother. How could I forget that? He would always watch out for me at school and walk me home." My lips quivered and tears flowed again as I looked at him. "I don't know how to deal with this, Travis. I want to hate him for what he did, but there's a part of me that misses the brother I knew, the brother I loved."

Travis pulled me in closer. "What you're going through is normal. I've watched you since Davin died, you've been suppressing your emotions and refusing to talk to anyone about it, and it's because you're confused about your feelings. You haven't been sure how to react. Your head is telling you that you should hate him because of the crimes he's committed, one of which was to Sabela, someone close to you, but yet your heart is telling you something different." He gave me a loving squeeze. "Don't be afraid to follow your heart, it's okay. He was your brother, and from what I just saw, you do have some fond memories of him. There was a time in your life you were proud of your older brother, right?"

I nodded and wiped away more tears. "Yes, I always looked up to him. We were inseparable. I may have been jealous of him because he always got what he wanted, and I'm not sure if it was my imagination, but I always felt mom and dad favored him."

Travis gave me a caring smile. "He was your mom and dad's first child as well as the eldest, so I'm sure they spoiled him as most parents do with their firstborn. Claire, you're dealing with so many mixed emotions, I understand why you shut down, I think I would have, too. It's what we do when we can't cope."

I sniffed back my runny nose. "Seeing this rock just opened up a floodgate of emotions. This may sound silly, but I don't want to leave this rock just yet. I'm afraid if I do the memories will fade, I need to remember Davin as a brother for a while."

"Sweetheart, take all the time you need, this is good for you. It's what you need to do, and I'm here for you."

I gave him another weak smile. "Thank you. You know, I've tried so hard to hate him, and a part of me does, but I can't ignore the fact that he was my brother, and I know he cared about me and loved me at some point. I just don't understand why he did the things he did." I leaned into Travis' body, feeling safe in his embrace. "I first began noticing a change in him when he was with Sabela - he couldn't stop talking about her, it was like he was possessed."

"Was Sabela his first girlfriend?" Travis asked.

I shook my head. "No, he'd had others, they were short-lived, and I got the impression they were just flings, but Sabela was different. He told me a few weeks after she'd moved in with him that he was going to marry her. Davin had never talked of marriage; his plan was to go to university and get his degree. I'd asked him if he'd talked to Sabela about marriage, but looking back at it now I thought at the time his reply to be odd, but I said nothing and brushed it off. Now I wished I'd have said something."

"What did he say?"

I took a deep breath, "he said you know me sis, I always get what I want. He sounded different, too, when he said it. Almost eerie. When he left for university, we grew apart and I rarely heard from him. It wasn't until I found out what he did to Sabela and the other girls that I felt ashamed to call him my brother for the first time. I just don't understand why he had to hurt those women, that's the part I can never forgive him for."

"And you should never have to. What he did was a terrible

thing; it's unforgivable, and he deserved to be behind bars, I know you agree with that."

"Yes, I do. I just miss having a brother who I could look up to and be proud of, there was a time I did. My only family now is you."

Travis hesitated before talking. "You have a mom and dad, too."

I quickly pulled away from his hold and stood before him, pulling my hair away from my face. "I can't talk about them right now, please don't bring them up, I'm ready to go; this is too much to deal with."

CHAPTER 7

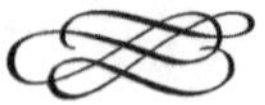

Travis

I regretted bringing up Claire's parents the minute I'd said it. She was finally opening up about Davin, and clearly it was too soon to deal with the anger she had towards her parents, how could I have been so stupid?

"I'm so sorry, Claire. I shouldn't have brought them up, forget what I said." I was afraid she'd shut down again and quickly tried to resume the conversation. "We don't have to leave, you need to talk about this; what you're doing will help you."

Claire ignored me and walked slowly down the rock. Once both feet were on the ground she turned and looked up at me, "please can we go now?"

My heart sank, I'd blown it. I released a heavy sigh. "Sure," I replied, climbing down the rock. "Do you want to keep walking this trail?"

"Yeah, it's pretty out here."

I took her hand and for the next ten minutes we walked in silence. I was unsure of what to say, afraid I may anger her or cause her to shut down again. These were fragile times for her, and I had to remind myself to let her deal with her emotions at her own pace.

We walked around a bend in the trail and Claire came to a sudden stop as she watched a squirrel run across the path in front of us, uttering a slight chuckle. "Davin used to chase the squirrels up into the tree."

My hand was still holding hers as I stood next to her. I didn't reply, I wanted her to continue with her memory.

"I think we were on this same path after we'd come down from the rock, mom and dad took us down this way. Davin and I went off the trail and played hide and seek between the trees. The trunks were enormous and great to hide behind, but when Davin saw a squirrel he would always come from behind the tree and chase it." She released a subtle smile. "I remember now - there was one squirrel that was much bigger than the other squirrels, he had a huge bushy grey tail and was super-friendly. We named him Toby and he'd follow us on the trail. Davin had a bag of peanuts and he'd drop some on the ground as we walked - Toby would follow us and eat every one of them."

She chuckled again but this time with misty eyes. As she looked up at the sky she said, "Oh, Davin, what happened to you? I'm sorry I wasn't there for you."

"He lost his way, Claire. There was nothing you could have done that would have helped him. You did nothing wrong and don't need to apologize."

She closed her eyes and furrowed her brow, "but I should have seen the signs, the way he was talking about Sabela, and the creepiness in his voice. I should have said something."

I reached out, grabbed her forearms and turned her around to face me. "Listen to me Claire, none of this is your fault. You were miles away from Davin, and you only found out about him attacking Sabela after it'd happened. Missing and mourning the brother that you knew and loved is okay and normal, but I won't allow you to be swallowed up with guilt, it will destroy not only you, but me, too. I love you Claire, mourn the loss of your brother, but please realize that Davin died because of what he did, not because you did nothing, there was nothing that you could've done."

Claire wiped away an escaped tear. "I love you too Travis, and I see you understand me and why I have tears for Davin, I'm just ashamed of myself."

I creased my brow. "Why?"

"Because it's one thing to talk to you, you're my husband. I could never share these memories and my grief for Davin with Sabela or the rest of our friends, not after what Davin did to her. She and the rest of our friends hate him, they'd never understand." Claire pulled away from my hold and spun around in frustration as she held her hand up to her brow. "How am I supposed to face them again and take their side by hating Davin? I just can't do that, Travis. He was my brother. I lost my brother, but I don't think they realize that. Their hatred stems from what he did, and I don't blame them, but it's much harder for me."

"Don't underestimate our friends. We've known them for a long time and have gone through a lot together. When Slater was in the hospital, he had some very kind words for you, don't forget that." I paused for a moment, "is that why you haven't talked to any of them about how you're feeling since Davin died? Are you afraid of their reaction?"

Claire looked at the ground and kicked the dirt. "Partly. I've been trying so hard to hate Davin so I can agree with their emotions, but I've realized that I can't. I hate him for what he did, but I can't hate the brother I grew up with. When I talk about my brother those are the memories of what I will tell people."

"And that's okay, Claire. When we get back home we're having a barbecue with everyone on moving day. I think that'd also be a suitable time to have an honest talk with them all so we can move on, what do you think?"

"I don't know, Travis. They're coming to help us, and if it weren't for Slater and Sabela we wouldn't even have the Children's home, I don't want to ruin it."

"Claire, Slater and Sabela are also our business partners; you can't work for them in this state of mind with the mixed feelings you have that also revolve around them. It may affect not only our friendship but our work relationship, too. I honestly think sharing what you're going through will help you deal with it better, as well as strengthen what we have with the two of them."

Claire nodded as she continued to look at the ground, then looked up into my eyes. "You're right. I need to do this. We'll talk with everyone at the barbecue."

CHAPTER 8

Claire

I wasn't expecting this trip to be so emotional and trigger so many forgotten memories. I just hoped I wasn't ruining it for Travis - after all, we're supposed to be on our honeymoon. But I couldn't block them out and pretend I remembered nothing, Travis was right, this is good for me, I need to be here to sort out my feelings and with his help try to heal myself.

We continued our walk down the path, hand-in-hand through the Giant Redwood Forest until I came to another abrupt stop and looked straight ahead.

Travis let go of my hand, "Claire, are you okay?"

I didn't answer and continued to look at the path ahead and saw myself as a little girl on the ground crying, my mom kneeling beside me. I was wrapped in her arms as she rocked me gently. My cries were loud, as if I was in pain. I looked off to the left of the path when I heard Davin call me. He was racing down the hillside between the giant trees, "Claire!" he screamed. My dad was waving to Davin and hollered, "over here son," standing over my mom as she continued to rock me.

It was all coming back to me now, we were still playing hide and seek. Davin had taken off up the hill as I stood on the trail and counted to 50. After I finished counting I bolted towards the hillside, tripping on a rock and falling down. I'd cut my knee open and there was quite a bit of blood. My mom insisted we leave so she could clean it up. "Jeffery, we need to go back to the hotel," she'd insisted. My dad wasn't too pleased with my mom's idea and tried to brush it off.

"She'll be fine Abigail, it's just a slight cut. Kids fall all the time, just give her a few minutes and she'll be okay," my dad argued.

I continued to stare ahead, watching the entire memory before me unfold. It seemed so real, Dad was right. But it wasn't until Davin returned, kneeling beside me and taking my hand that I felt better. "Sis, what happened? Can you walk?"

I smiled at Davin and nodded, then suddenly felt better when he was next to me. "Yes, I think so, can you help me get up?"

My mom released me from her embrace and allowed Davin to pull me up. "There you go, sis. I'll walk with you in case you fall again."

My dad took credit for not going back to the hotel, but looking back, Davin was the one who'd helped me and even stayed with me after my fall, as any good big brother would have. I never realized how much I'd depended on him.

As I turned to Travis who'd been silent this whole time, I took his hand and said, "I'm sorry. All these memories keep flooding back."

Travis squeezed my hand., "it's okay; like I said, it's good that you're remembering."

"Yeah, I guess you're right. I wish we didn't have to leave this afternoon, it'd be wonderful to stay here and see what other memories come flooding back. I feel such a connection here and I don't want it to end."

Travis surprised me with his reply, "then let's stay."

"Stay? How? We're supposed to drive to Yosemite today; besides, where would we camp? We only had the campground for one night," I pointed out.

Travis chuckled. "Claire, we can do whatever we want. Yosemite was an idea not a definite plan. If you need to stay here, then we'll stay."

"But where?"

"We can go outside the park, find a spot off the road and come back to the park tomorrow. Remember, we're winging it."

"You wouldn't object to staying the whole week? I just need to be here, and I'm sorry, I know this is your honeymoon, too."

Travis took me in his arms. "I wasn't looking forward to driving for hours to Yosemite anyway, and I love your idea. It's beautiful here, and if it's okay with you I'd love to hear more of your childhood memories, they're much better than mine."

CHAPTER 9

Travis

When Claire suggested we stay at the Redwoods, I couldn't agree fast enough. When I saw how it enabled her to open up and talk about Davin, the thought crossed my mind earlier in the day. We had the rest of our lives to go to Yosemite, this was more important.

"Do you want to stay here for a while, or do you want to keep walking?" I asked Claire as she gazed up at the trees.

She turned and faced me, "I'm getting hungry. We have some snacks in the backpack, let's stop for a bit and eat something."

"Sounds good." I pointed to a flat area underneath one of the giant trees, "how about over there?"

"Perfect," Claire replied, followed by a cute smile.

While we were eating our lunch, I felt comfortable probing Claire with more questions. She seemed more confident and showed a willingness to share more. I was seeing a change in her. "Do you know how long you were here with Davin and your parents?"

Claire shook her head. "No, I was so young. It must have been when school was out, and I'm sure we drove here from San Diego." She looked at me before taking a bite of her granola bar. "You know, I never remember camping with my mom and dad, I wonder why I liked it so much? Mom was not the outdoorsy type. Whenever we went someplace we always stayed in a hotel."

"Well, I think it's because you like being independent. Sounds to me like Davin was raised under your parents' wing and you needed to prove yourself a lot, and camping became a part of that for you. A young single woman camping alone in the wilderness, that takes guts and strength, Claire."

"I never looked at it that way, I just love being outdoors."

"How about Davin? Did he enjoy camping as much as you did?"

Claire cracked a laugh "oh, hell no. He was like mom and dad, he had to stay in the best hotels and eat at the best restaurants, paid for by mom and dad of course."

"See, that's what I mean. He never had to prove himself to anyone, you did. Even climbing that rock back there, you had to overcome your fears."

"I never gave it much thought, but it all makes sense now." Claire threw her empty wrapper into the backpack, "okay, that's enough food. How about we take a drive out of the park and find a place to camp? I don't want to be setting up in the dark."

"But you've hardly eaten."

"My pants are getting tight, I'm on a diet," she giggled, patting her stomach.

"On a diet? You're fine. You don't need to diet."

Claire stood and finished her bottle of water. "No, these pants feel much tighter. Come on, let's go."

I shook my head. "Well, I think your body is perfect," I said, taking her hand.

We spent the next few hours driving around admiring the glorious scenery and looking for a place to camp, occasionally pulling over and taking short hikes. Claire found the perfect spot next to a creek just off the dirt road.

"This is perfect," Claire said, breathing in the fresh air and smiling. "We can bring the truck down here and park it right under that tree," she said, pointing.

I scanned the area. I didn't see any private road signs or gates. "Yeah, this'll work," giving her a devious grin, "we can even go skinny dipping in the creek tonight. It looks deep enough." I knelt down and put my fingers in the water, "and the temperature is perfect, wonder if there's any fish in it? I brought fishing poles."

"And we have plenty of bottled water for the night. We can go into town tomorrow and restock our supplies," Claire confirmed, giving me a huge smile.

"Come on, let's go get the truck. I'm excited."

Over the next few hours, we set up camp and decided it would be sardines and bread for dinner. Neither one of us felt comfortable having a campfire in the middle of the forest nor did we want to cook.

"The nights are pretty warm, we should be fine," I told Claire, putting the last peg in the ground for the tent.

"And if it's not I'll just snuggle up close to you," Claire said, rubbing her body against mine.

I took her in my arms and kissed her passionately on the lips. "It's so good to see you smiling again and finally being honest with your feelings. I was worried that you regretted marrying me," I said, followed up by a sarcastic laugh.

Claire gave me a friendly slap on my chest. "You know it was never about you, but I do owe you a big thank you."

Still locked in my embrace, I swayed her body gently from side-to-side. "Thank me for what?"

"For knowing me better than I do, and for helping me get to where I am right now with all the crap that's happened." I rolled my eyes, "this is exactly what you did when I fell out with my parents the first time, you're rather good at this."

I laughed. "No, I just know that talking through our feelings is the best medicine, it never fails, I've had to do it a lot with my past and upbringing." I pushed and knew I was treading on fragile ground but went ahead with it anyway. "It worked with your parents back then, it may work again."

Claire broke away from my hold, creating distance between us. "Please don't go there, Travis, I told you I can't think about them right now, I'm dealing with Davin."

I took a step towards her, she took a step back. I knew I was pushing her, but I couldn't stop myself and held out my hand which she ignored. "You're going to have to face it sometime, Claire. You made amends before with them, I just know you can do it again."

She raised her hands and closed her eyes, her brow furled. "Don't Travis," she yelled, storming off towards the tent.

Dust kicked up from under her hiking boots as she neared the tent and entered. "Claire, can we talk about this?"

"No, Travis. I'm done. I'm not going there," she hollered from inside the tent.

I leaned against the truck and kicked the dirt beneath my feet, hissing, "Damn it." I'd pushed her too far and may have blown everything we'd accomplished; she may never want to talk about Davin or her parents again. I can't let her shut down once more.

CHAPTER 10

Claire

Tears pooled in my eyes but I refused to let them fall, I would not cry over my parents, they didn't deserve any pity from me. If it wasn't for them Davin would probably still be in jail, better yet, alive. I blamed them for his death. He would have had time to sit in jail and think about what he'd done, and perhaps be the brother I once knew when he came out. But no, my mother had to tell him Sabela was getting married and now he's dead.

I dropped to my knees and buried my face in my palms, realizing I would never know if Davin could have changed his ways. And then it hit me like a thunderstorm - all the things I would never experience with him because of his death. My emotions were in turmoil, which was what I'd been so afraid of. I'm so overwhelmed with grief and anger I couldn't handle it.

Many 'what ifs' circled in my head; Davin may have eventually found the right woman and gotten married, I would never have a sister-in-law or be an aunt to his children who would have been my nieces and nephews. The memories I had today of us as kids can never be shared with him and then, just as quickly anger took over.

I switched from feeling saddened by what I would never have to feeling anger and crying out loud. "Why Davin?" I sobbed. "Why did you do what you did? Why were you so obsessed with Sabela? Why did you hurt those other women? I hate you for what you did. Sabela is my friend; you hurt her, and I can never forgive you for that. How am I supposed to go on missing you as a brother, but hate you and feel ashamed of you? I feel like I'm being pulled in all directions, and I don't know how to react." I didn't know I was yelling out loud to myself until I heard Travis' voice outside the tent.

"Claire, are you okay?"

I didn't answer and remained on my knees.

"Claire, can I come in? I'm sorry, okay? I know this is hard for you. Please don't shut me out, I love you."

I didn't want him to see me in this state, I needed to pull myself together. I pulled my hair away from my face and stood. "Give me a few minutes, I'll be right out."

"Okay, I'll be next to the truck."

I stood motionless, holding my breath as I heard his footsteps walking away from the tent.

After wiping my moist cheeks and giving my head a good shake to compose myself, I exited the tent with my hands clasped together to hide their shaking. Travis took a few steps towards me with a sadness in his eyes. "I hate seeing you hurting like this, what can I do? I feel so helpless."

We stood six feet away from each other; Travis had stopped walking, unsure if I was going to push him away if he came any closer.

"I don't know, Travis, this is all too much. Everything is just hitting me all at once and I don't know how to deal with it. When you brought up my parents, I felt nothing but rage towards them, I still do, and I blame my mom for everything. It's because of her that Davin is dead," I yelled.

Travis couldn't hide his shock and took two more steps toward me, "Claire, Davin is to blame not your parents, he's the one who threatened Sabela, no one is to blame but him."

I disagreed and shook my head vigorously. "No, Travis, if she had said nothing to him, he would still be alive today."

"Claire, he would have found out eventually, and who knows what he would have done? He would have found a way to escape and find her, we both know that. Your mom loved him, just as she loves you. She wanted to share your special day with him, she didn't know he would react the way he did." He held out his hand, "come on you've been doing so well, I messed up bringing up your parents and I'm sorry. Right now, you're mourning the loss of your brother, let's just get through that, okay? Do you want to go back to the Redwoods tomorrow?"

This time I took a few steps towards him until I could feel his cool breath on my lips. I said nothing and leaned in to kiss him. He immediately embraced me in his arms, "I'm so sorry, you're the last person I should be releasing my anger and frustrations on, you've been my pillar of strength through this whole damn thing." My head rested on his shoulder, "I'm trying to sort out all the crap that's going on in my head, I'll try to do a better job with it."

"You don't have to apologize to anyone, especially me." He gazed into my eyes and gave me a caring smile. "How about we don't talk about Davin or your parents for the rest of the night? The sun will go down soon, let's fix dinner, then we can go skinny dipping in the creek under the moon and stars."

I smiled. "Sounds perfect," I said as I broke away and walked over to the back of the truck, sliding the ice chest onto the tailgate.

An hour later after we'd feasted on sardines, bread rolls and apples, Travis stood and undressed. "I'll race you to the creek," he hollered, balancing on one leg to take off his jeans.

I laughed as he hopped around on one leg as I pulled my T-shirt over my head. "You're on," I laughed, tossing my T-shirt on the ground and quickly unzipping my jeans as I took a seat to pull them off.

After successfully removing his jeans, Travis hastily stripped his body of the rest of his clothes and ran towards the creek. "I'll see you in the water."

I was a few minutes behind him and dove into the creek, breaking the surface of the water with a shriek. "Man, this water is cold!" I screamed, my lips shivering and my body stiffening.

Travis cracked a laugh, "give it a minute, you'll get used to it."

I swam around to warm my body up from the chilled water and within minutes my muscles relaxed as my body adapted to the frigid temperature.

"See, it feels good, doesn't it?" Travis called from across the creek.

I flipped over on my back and floated, splashing my hands. "It does," I gasped, looking up at the now dark skies. "Oh Travis, lay on your back and look at the stars, it's amazing."

Travis swam over to me and when he was close, he floated onto his back and looked up. "Wow! That's incredible! Look at the moon, it's so bright."

For a few moments the beauty above and the sound of the surrounding water mesmerized me. "I'm in heaven," I whispered as Travis maneuvered his body closer to mine and caressed me beneath the water. Floating on my back with my breasts peeking above the surface, Travis tickled me between my legs and kneaded my stomach with long sensual strokes before massaging my breasts. I moaned from his touch and continued to tread water as Travis seduced me with his hands, kicking the water to stay afloat.

Within a few minutes I wanted more, and I smiled at Travis, "follow me," I whispered in a sultry voice, flipping my body over and swimming over to shallower water near the banks. Travis swam close behind me, and when I could touch the creek bottom, I stood up and raised my hands above my head. Only my thighs were hidden beneath the water, the rest of my wet, naked body glimmered from the moonlight above us. Travis stood, exposing his nakedness from the knees up - he looked magnificent. His body was firm, and the water ran down every muscle as he rose out of the water. I watched with desire as he shook his drenched hair and approached me, taking me into his arms. We were hungry for each other and kissed with electrifying passion, our hands exploring each other's bodies with fiery strokes and caresses. Our moans were loud and echoed through the tall pine trees, but we didn't care, we were alone in the forest with nature, feeling wild.

Travis groped every exposed surface of my skin as we continued to kiss hard before he guided me to a large, flat rock at the edge of the creek. I needed no instructions; I laid down on the rough surface so he could take me. I breathed in deeply as he lowered his body onto mine and slid his arms behind my back to protect me from the rock. Drips of water from his hair trickled down my face as he slowly entered and rode me slowly. I closed my eyes and released a loud moan of satisfaction as we reached a climax in the wilderness, and when we both came, we howled like wolves.

CHAPTER 11

Claire

We woke up to the sound of singing birds outside and the heat of the morning sun penetrating the tent's canvas. I rolled over and snuggled up to Travis, resting my head on his bare chest as he leaned in and kissed the top of my head.

"Hey beautiful," he whispered, followed by a yawn.

"Hey," I whispered back. "You want to get dressed and go into town for breakfast? I'm dying for a cup of coffee, and I don't want to cook anything out here."

"Sure, I could use a cup myself, then we'll head back into the park."

I smiled and gave his chest a light pat, "that'd be nice. I'm going to go outside, find a place to pee and grab our toothbrushes from the truck," I chuckled, pulling myself out of the sleeping bag and putting on a pair of shorts and a T-shirt.

I stepped out of the tent and stretched my tired body, my

muscles ached from all the walking we did yesterday, so I did a few leg-bends to loosen them up. I looked up in the sky and guessed it was around 8:00 AM from where the sun sat in the sky as I headed towards the creek to take a pee. Not wanting to wander off too far from our campsite, I found the perfect spot at the edge of the creek and took a squat after pulling down my shorts.

When I returned to camp Travis was nowhere to be found; I assumed he was still in the tent as I headed over to the truck to grab our toiletry bag. It was then that I came to a sudden stop about 50 feet from the truck and froze. I gasped, feeling my heart hammer beneath my chest as I watched in shock as a California black bear weighing around 700 pounds stood in the bed of our truck. Relieved that his back faced me I remained still, then the bear threw a saucepan onto the ground and picked up another from inside a plastic tote without a matching lid. "Fuck!" I whispered under my breath as another saucepan landed on the ground with a loud crash.

Still frozen, I scanned the area wide eyed without moving my head. "Where's Travis?" I whispered harshly. A loud crash startled me, and I gasped a little too loud for comfort. The bear had picked up one of the totes and thrown it over the side of the truck. I watched as it smashed to the ground, plastic pieces from the shattered tote, dishes and paper plates scattered on the ground. "Thank god we took all the food inside the tent last night," I whispered to myself as the bear grabbed my canvas bag full of clothes, and then with one swipe of his massive claws he ripped the bag open like it was a piece of paper. "No, not my clothes..." I remained frozen to the ground, hands at my sides. My mind was racing as I contemplated what to do. "Travis, where the fuck are you?" Afraid to take my eyes off the bear or turn my back on him, I remained motionless as he pulled out a pair of my jeans and tossed them onto the ground, then I heard a ripping sound, it was my favorite sage green T-shirt. The bear held it with his two front paws and shredded it before tossing it aside. "Oh, this is not good, I'll have no clothes if he keeps this up," I mumbled under my breath. Thankfully the bear still had his back to me and was unaware of my presence as I racked my brain trying to think of what I had to do next. I was defenseless, I'd left the pepper spray in the tent. Stupid me! I had nothing to defend myself with or any way to make a loud noise to scare him off.

Suddenly, I thought I heard my name, "Claire!" It was a sharp whisper, "don't turn around, I'm in the tent."

I pinned my ears towards him, slowly nodding my head so that he knew I'd heard him.

He spoke again in a sharp whisper, "do not make any sudden moves, slowly walk back towards the tent without taking your eyes off the bear."

I held my breath and nodded again, then stared straight at the bear as I took one step backward and then another.

"Okay, that's good, you're about 30 feet from the tent. Take two more steps," Travis instructed.

I gave a slight nod and remained focused on the bear who'd thrown my bag on the ground and now had Travis' bag. I took two more steps back and paused as my heart continued to race.

"That's good," Travis whispered. "You're doing great. Now, take two more steps."

I held my breath and slowly moved my left leg behind me. God I wished I was inside the tent with Travis. I moved my right leg and managed to hold back a horrifying shriek as I heard a branch break beneath my foot, "fuck!" I instantly froze, fearing the bear may have heard it but he was making so much noise destroying our stuff that he hadn't. I remained motionless for a moment before attempting to take a few more steps backward.

"You're almost here," Travis whispered, "another 15 feet."

My heart continued to race as my breathing elevated and my palms began to sweat. I continued to look ahead at the bear who was now at the front of the bed of our truck peering into the cab through the rear window. I watched in horror as he stood on his hind legs and raised his front paws, he was huge, towering over the cab. With tremendous force he brought his paws down onto the roof of the cab and punched it hard.

Travis reacted first, "shit!"

My eyes were wide as I watched the bear pound the roof of the truck again. It shook from the impact, and I saw a massive dent in the roof from where I stood. "Holy shit!" I gasped beneath my breath, then froze again as the bear continued to pound on the truck.

"Take a few more steps back while the bear is making noise," Travis instructed.

I nodded and resumed walking back slowly.

"That's it, you're almost here. Slowly reach out behind you so I can grab your hand."

Yearning to feel the security of his grasp, I slowly extended my hand behind me and continued to take small steps backwards.

Within a few minutes I felt his hand and clutched it.

"Okay, a few more steps, come on babe," Travis urged me.

I released a huge sigh of relief when Travis grabbed my arm, pulled me inside the tent and held me close. I rested my head on his chest and felt his heart pounding. Wrapping my hands around his waist, he engulfed me in his arms and squeezed my body tight. "Oh god, I've never been so scared in my life, that bear is huge," I gasped with bated breath.

"He's frigging massive, he's destroying my truck."

We remained inside the tent locked in each other's arms as the bear continued to invade our truck. "What are we going to do?" I asked, panicking.

"We're going to stay in here and just wait; pretty soon he'll realize there's no food in the truck and hopefully move on without doing too much more damage."

"The food's in here, what if he comes towards the tent?"

Travis let me go for a few seconds, grabbed the two cans of bear spray next to the sleeping bag and handed me one. "Hold on to this and if he comes towards the tent, we both aim the bear spray at him and make as much noise as we can."

My hands shook as I took the spray and held it tight before embracing Travis' hold again.

I'm not sure how long we remained locked in each other's arms while the bear continued to rummage through our belongings, but it seemed like an eternity, then we heard a loud thud. Travis let go of me then tiptoed to the small gap in the tent's entrance and peeked out. "He's out of the truck and sniffing all of our stuff on the ground." Travis held his breath for a few seconds and then spoke again, "he's looking over at the forest."

"He's not coming this way, is he?" I questioned.

Travis shook his head. "No, he's walking around to the front of the truck and he's on his hind legs looking over the hood."

"Shit! I hope he doesn't damage the front end."

"Now he's back on all fours and walking away from the truck. I think he's heading towards the creek," Travis whispered with some hope.

"Oh god, I hope so," I gasped.

Travis continued to peek outside the tent. "Yes, he's walking away, and he's heading for the creek, I guess he worked up a thirst. We're going to stay in here for a while and make sure he's gone."

We remained in the tent for a good fifteen minutes. The silence outside was welcoming, but we wanted to make sure the bear would not return after he'd quenched his thirst. "Okay, I think the coast is clear, let's go see what the damage is," Travis said, taking my hand and leading me out of the tent.

Travis continued to hold my hand as we slowly made our way over to the truck, constantly checking our surroundings for any sight of the bear. There was none, and my heart rate slowly returned to normal.

"Look at this mess," I shrieked as we neared the truck. "There's nothing left in the truck bed." I picked up some of my clothes that were scattered on the ground, the bear's sharp claws had shredded a lot of them. "He ruined most of my clothes."

Travis held up a pair of what had once been a pair of jeans and was now a tattered piece of denim. "Mine too." He walked over to a tote that was upside down and flipped it over. Shattered flashlights and batteries lay scattered on the ground. "Wow, what a mess," he said, jumping up into the bed of the truck. A coffee cup rolled to the other side of the truck bed as he walked towards the cab and inspected the roof where the bear had pounded on it. "Wow, he sure did a number on this, there's a massive dent."

I jumped up into the bed and joined him in the cab. The bear had caved in the entire middle of the roof. I swept my hand across the dent, "damn, it's amazing how strong they are, at least we can still sit inside the cab."

"Yeah, I'll take it to a body shop when we get home. They should be able to knock that out." Travis scanned the mess around the truck. "I'm not sure how much of this we can save, let's clean it up, pack up the tent and head into town, I need a big breakfast."

I jumped off the truck and located the roll of trash bags that had escaped from one of the totes and began tossing the ruined clothes and other items inside it. "Sounds good, so far I'm finding more trash than salvageable items," I stated. "We may have to cut this trip short."

CHAPTER 12

Claire

It took us a good hour to clean up the mess around the truck. When we were done, we had four bags of trash comprised of clothes, dented pots and pans, dirty and destroyed cups and plates, along with shattered flashlights and broken totes. I held up a handful of clothes that weren't damaged and a few toiletries, "this is all I have, what about you?" I asked Travis, who was on the other side of the truck collecting more trash.

"Not much except a few pairs of jeans, a T-shirt and my fishing tackle and rods."

I cringed when I found two of my books underneath the truck, "oh man, he tore up my books, I was really enjoying those," I moaned, kneeling down and reaching under the truck.

Travis walked over to where I stood, added his pile of good stuff to mine and threw the trash bags in the back of the truck. "There's a small store in town where we could probably buy supplies and some clothes if we're going to stay a few more days."

"Yes, let's check it out, I'm not ready to leave yet. For whatever reason I feel really close to Davin here and I don't want to lose that moment just yet. I'm afraid when we get home he'll just become a distant memory. This is helping me sort through all of the mixed emotions I'm feeling."

Travis stood before me and smiled, resting his hands on my shoulders. "Take all the time you need." He squeezed my shoulders, "come on, let's go get some breakfast and then we'll check out the store for supplies."

Over breakfast we relived our encounter with the bear, sharing the fear and just how powerless we felt.

"I thought seeing the mama bear with her cubs crossing the road when we first arrived in the park was an amazing experience, but my god, the bear at our campsite was massive, I felt totally defenseless. If he had come at me, I wouldn't have stood a chance," I said.

"I never want to be that close to a bear ever again," Travis admitted, eyes wide.

After a huge breakfast grill with the works we headed over to the store a half mile away and felt we'd scored as we discovered a rack of T-shirts, sweatpants and shorts.

"We should get a commission for advertising this little town for the next few days," Travis laughed, grabbing a handful of T-shirts. "All these clothes have the town's name on them."

I held up one of the price tags, "these aren't cheap either, this is really going to cut into our budget," I moaned.

Travis took the clothes I had draped over my arm and walked over to the counter where we'd placed some canned food and other necessities. "Okay, that'll do it," Travis told the clerk.

"Wait, I found these three totes we can put everything in," I suggested. The clerk took them from my hands and filled them with our purchase.

"That will be $389.15," the clerk said with a courteous smile.

Our jaws dropped as Travis reached for his wallet in his back pocket. "Wow! I guess there'll be no fancy dinners for us for the rest of this trip," he said, handing over his credit card.

"You've got that right. It's going to be cold sandwiches for lunch, and beans and bread for dinner," I joked, grabbing one of the totes.

It didn't take us long to drive to Sequoia National Park and find a place to park. Travis pulled out the two new backpacks and started filling them up with water and snacks as I found the ready-made sandwiches.

"I don't want any fresh food left in this truck while we're not here. The canned goods should be fine, and I'll put the three totes and the ice chest with just water in it in the cab. We got lucky the last time we were here."

"Don't worry, the crackers and sandwiches are going with us and everything else is in cans," I told him.

Once everything was secure Travis locked the truck and adjusted the straps on my backpack until they were snug. "Is that better?" he asked.

I shook my body and slid my hands under the straps. "Yes, thanks," I told him, taking his hand. The weather was a few degrees warmer than the previous day and I was feeling it after walking for a while. Beads of sweat formed on my forehead, and I could feel a headache coming on.

"Do you mind if we stop for a while? I'm not feeling too good."

Travis immediately stopped and looked into my eyes. "What's wrong?" he said, placing his hand on my forehead. "Oh wow, you're sweating." He took my hand and led me off the trail. "Come on, let's go sit under a tree."

I waited while Travis unrolled the blanket tied to his backpack and laid it on the ground. He patted it, "here you go."

The weight of the backpack felt like it had doubled in the brief time we'd been hiking, and I quickly removed it before taking a seat on the blanket. My head was spinning and my headache had become excruciatingly painful. "I have to lie down," I moaned, holding my brow.

Travis took my backpack and placed it under my head "here, rest your head on this. Are you going to be okay?"

"Yeah, I think it's the heat, I just need to rest for a while."

" Are you sure? This isn't like you, the heat never bothered you before." He took my hand. "Is it just your head? Anywhere else hurt?" Travis asked, as I continued to hold my brow.

I lowered my hand to my abdomen, "my stomach's upset; I wonder if I ate some bad food at the restaurant?"

"We both had the same breakfast, so I doubt it. I hope you're going to be okay?"

To fight off the pain I felt in my head as well as the nausea I spoke through gritted teeth. "I'll be fine, I just need a few minutes." And then it hit me; with a sense of urgency, I quickly stood while embracing my stomach. "Oh shit, I'm going to throw up," I cried as I ran away from the blanket and behind a tree close by. Within seconds, my breakfast was on the ground at my feet. I gagged at the vile taste left behind in my mouth as I felt another round of vomit travel up my throat. "Oh god," I cried out loud as I threw up the rest of my breakfast. Still leaning over, I wiped my mouth and coughed a few times to get the disgusting taste out of my mouth. "Travis, can you bring me some water, please?" I called, still bent over.

"Yes! Hang on, I'll be right there," he said with urgency.

After chugging almost a whole bottle of water, I took a few deep breaths and returned to the blanket where Travis hugged me. I rested my head on his chest and closed my eyes, "god I feel like crap," I moaned, holding my stomach.

"Let's just stay here for a while and let you rest, hopefully you'll feel better soon," he said, placing his hand on my forehead. "Do you have a fever?"

"I don't think so."

"Nope, you don't."

As I lay in Travis' arms, thoughts of the Children's home entered my mind. "Do you think we're going to be good parents to the kids that come to the home?"

Travis squeezed my shoulder. "Of course we are. Why wouldn't we be? We've worked really hard for this."

"I know, but we've never been parents before."

Travis chuckled, "and neither have any first-time parents. Why all the silly doubts and questions?"

"I don't know, I guess because I've been thinking a lot about Davin on this trip, and I partially blame my parents for giving him everything he wanted and ruining him. I just don't want to be like them and make the same mistakes with the children we're supposed to be giving a second chance in life to."

"And you won't, you're nothing like your parents. You made sure of that by carving out your own path in life and being strong and independent, it's one of the things I love about you." He released another chuckle. "And besides, we'll be raising these kids together and making all the decisions as a team. We're going to be great parents, okay?"

"Thanks, I'm just worrying too much, this trip has been nothing but a roller coaster of emotions."

"Yes, but it's all good, I think it's what you needed. When we get back we'll have a discussion with Slater and Sabela, and you can finally be honest about what you're going through."

"Yeah, I'm not looking forward to that, but you're right, if we're going to be working together I can't have this hovering over my head."

"Everything's going to be fine, they're both reasonable and very understanding people. I'm sure they'll understand that you have mixed emotions about Davin, and you can't completely hate him."

I released a heavy sigh. "God, I hope you're right and that it doesn't jeopardize everything we've worked for."

CHAPTER 13

Claire

We remained under the shade of the Giant Sequoia trees for the next few hours. My stomach was still upset, but the urge to vomit had subsided, much to my relief. As I lay in Travis' arms, I shared more childhood memories of Davin and I playing here at the park, it felt good to reminisce about my relationship with my brother and what I'd forgotten.

Travis picked up his phone and glanced at the screen, "it's almost three o'clock, do you want to go to a restaurant and get an early dinner, then figure out where we're going to camp for the night? I don't think I want to go back to the creek with that bear hanging out."

I cringed, "oh, don't even mention food, I still feel queasy. Just the thought of putting anything in my stomach makes me nauseous."

"Well, that's not good," he said, with a caring smile, "tell you what - why don't we get a room at the Inn tonight? We'll put you in a nice comfy bed where you can get plenty of rest." He nudged my arm, "hey, you could even take a bath if the room has a tub, I really don't like the idea of you sleeping on the ground when you're not feeling well."

"Thanks, I'd like that, and we can grab something for you to eat from the store or the restaurant."

"As long as me eating in front of you doesn't make you nauseous."

"I should be fine."

"Okay then, let's pack up and head into town."

Travis ordered fish and chips from the restaurant, and while we waited for his order, he called up the Inn, and to our relief got us a room for the night.

"Oh, thank god," I said, releasing an enormous sigh of relief. "I wasn't looking forward to setting up camp and tossing and turning in the sleeping bag. This was a good idea you had, I'm looking forward to laying on a soft mattress and watching a movie with you."

"I agree. Hey, I'm going to call my mom and check in, do you want to say hi?"

"Of course I do, and I want to hear how Tilly's doing, I sure miss her."

Travis put his phone on speaker so we could both talk with her, Travis smiled when he heard her voice. "Hey mom, it's your favorite son. How are things going, and how's Tilly?"

"Hi, Travis, everything's going well, Tilly is such a wonderful dog, and she's splendid company."

Suddenly Tilly interrupted our conversation with a loud bark and I laughed out loud. "Hey Tilly, mama misses you!"

Caroline joined in on the laughter. "I have you on speaker, she must hear your voices."

I raised my hand to my heart at the sound of Tilly's cries. "Aww, thank you for taking care of her, we're staying at an Inn tonight, I'll let Travis give you the phone number in case you need to get in touch with us, we don't have cell phone service, see you soon."

After ending the call with Caroline, the waitress soon appeared with Travis' food, the odor of it coming out of the brown bag instantly turned my stomach. "Oh, jeez," I moaned, holding my nose.

Travis rested his hand on my shoulder as I took a step back, "are you okay?"

"Yeah sorry, the smell of your food just made me a little nauseous, I'll be okay."

"Do you want me to eat it here?" Travis asked, grabbing his bag.

I shook my head, "no, it's fine. Let's go to the Inn, I'll leave if it bothers me," I joked.

Being such a small town, it only took us five minutes to drive to the Inn. Travis parked in front of the entrance and reached over to the back seat where he'd covered his food with his jacket so the smell wouldn't bother me.

I remained seated, staring at the building in front of me, not noticing as Travis stepped out of the truck.

"Claire, are you coming?" Travis said from outside the truck.

I didn't reply but remained focused on the building, my body went limp.

"Claire?" Travis repeated.

I ignored him. "I've been here before; this must have been where we stayed with mom and dad."

Travis got back in the truck, "are you sure?"

My eyes remained locked on the Inn, and I nodded. "Yes, I'm positive. The paint color may be different, but the building is exactly how I remember it." I pointed to the left of the office, "and that giant rooster statue was there when we were here, Dad even took a picture of Davin and I standing next to it, I wonder if he still has it?"

Travis turned his head and looked at the rooster, "wow, I guess it's no surprise that you stayed here. There aren't many inns and hotels around, especially one with a giant rooster." He turned and looked at me, and I finally acknowledged him. "Are you okay staying here?" he asked.

I gave him a weak smile. I still wasn't feeling well, and the thought of looking for another place didn't sound appealing. "Yes, it's fine, but it may ignite more childhood memories."

Travis nodded. "Okay then, let's go check in, I can come back down for our bags."

The room overlooked the creek, and it thrilled me to find a small outside deck with a bistro table and two chairs outside on the small deck. I immediately opened the sliding glass door and stepped outside to enjoy the incredible view. "This view is amazing," I called to Travis, who was setting his food up on the table in the room. Still holding a plastic fork he joined me on the deck and embraced me in his arms. "Wow! This is awesome, why don't you sit out here while I eat? I don't want you getting sick again."

"You don't have to ask me twice, I could sit here all day."

By the time the sun was setting and I'd had a relaxing warm bath, I felt better and snuggled with Travis on the bed to watch a movie. But a half hour in, I fell asleep in his arms and woke up to Travis calling my name.

"Claire, wake up! You're having a nightmare!"

I shook my body and waved my arms, "don't touch me."

I felt hands on my shoulders. "Claire, it's Travis, wake up, it's just a dream."

I shook my head vigorously. "No! Stop touching me." I opened my eyes and stared at Travis. Tears poured down my face and my body shook as I threw myself into his arms.

Travis held me tight as my body continued to shake. "Sweetheart, it's okay, you just had a bad dream."

I covered my face, my hands trembling, sweat seeping from my brow, "he was in my bed touching me," I cried.

"Claire honey, it was just a dream, no one is in your bed, you're here with me."

I pulled away from Travis' embrace. My voice broke as I tried to tell him, and I couldn't stop my body from shaking. "It was Davin, we were at this Inn and he was in my bed. Travis, he touched me, I was his sister; what does this mean?"

CHAPTER 14

Travis

I was numb from Claire's words. Did Davin molest his own sister? "Claire, are you sure it was Davin in your dream?"

Claire leaned into me and rested her head on my chest. My heart rate elevated after what she'd told me.

"Yes, I'm sure." She creased her brow and closed her eyes in despair. "It seemed so real. I know he did it, I just know it. We shared a room here with twin beds. Mom and dad slept in the adjoining room. I remember clearly now after the lights were out, he snuck into my bed and told me to be quiet." She looked at me with fear in her eyes. "Travis, he was naked."

Suddenly Claire's body jolted, and she broke away from my hold and jumped out of bed. "I don't want to remember anymore. All I know is that Davin did some things that he shouldn't have done. He was a monster long before he attacked Sabela and those other girls, and I hate him, Travis. I fucking hate him! I'm glad he's dead."

Claire's words shattered my heart, but it all made sense why she never dated much and had a hard time trusting men, how could she? I watched with misty eyes as Claire fell to her knees and sobbed. Should I approach her? What if she pushes me away? I slowly stood from the bed and made my way over to her, her sobs tearing at my heart. I knelt beside her and cautiously wrapped my arm across her shoulders. "It's okay Claire, I'm here. No one is going to hurt you anymore."

"Why did he do it? I don't understand Travis, I was his baby sister."

"He was a sick person, even at an early age. There's a reason why you didn't remember, you didn't want to."

Claire rubbed her swollen red eyes and looked at me. "Were there other times I wonder? How many times did he do this?"

I took her in my arms. "Does it matter? One, two, three times. It should never have happened even once. Don't torture yourself, you were a little girl."

Claire grabbed my arm and used it to pull herself up. "I want to go home."

I stood to meet her gaze. "Now? You want to go home now?"

"Yes, I don't want to spend another minute in this awful place. I want to get as far away as possible. Please, can we go home? I want to sleep in my bed with you and Tilly." Her hand trembled as she held it out. "Give me the keys. I'll meet you in the truck. I need to get out of here," she insisted while dressing with urgency.

I reached into my front pocket and handed her my keys. "I'll be as quick as I can."

She nodded and left the room in silence with her head hung low. Left alone, I was still numb from Claire's latest discovery of her childhood. "What a bastard," I hissed under my breath as I gathered our things and tossed them in the bag. I noticed Claire's cell phone on the end table and put it in her purse which she'd left on the bed. Within minutes I was satisfied I had packed everything and left the Inn key card on the small desk before turning off the lights and leaving the room.

I found Claire sitting on the passenger side of the truck, her knees bent up under her chin and her head buried. Her sobs were loud, and I had no words to comfort her. All I could do was be there for her and not allow her to blame any of Davin's wrongdoings on herself.

I eased into the truck and slid closer to her, cautiously placing my hand on her thigh. "Hey, do you want me to hold you?"

She nodded without looking at me or raising her head and slid her body closer to mine, resting her head in my lap. Her tears continued, and I rubbed her back to soothe her. "It's going to be okay Claire, I love you."

She remained silent and continued to cry in my lap as my heart ached for the pain she was feeling. I felt helpless and wanted so much to make all of this go away.

Claire's tears subsided, but I continued to rub her back as she repositioned her head in my lap, then she spoke. "Why did he do it, Travis? Did I make him do it?"

What I feared was happening, and I pulled Claire up and shook her shoulders gently, giving her a hard stare. "No, Claire! Don't you ever think that! You were an innocent young girl, this is no fault of yours. Your brother was obviously not well at an early age and hid it well. We will never know why that was or who else he may have hurt. You're not responsible for any of his actions." I shook her shoulders. I needed to get through to her. "Do you understand me? You're not to blame for any of this."

She released a cruel, sarcastic laugh. "He sure had us fooled, especially mom and dad. God, he could do no wrong in their eyes." She took a deep breath and held my hand. "It was wrong of me to blame them for his death. Davin died because he was a monster, I just didn't want to believe it."

"It's okay, there's so much to understand. You are now discovering the truth and working through it all." I gave her a caring smile. "Are you ready to go home? You can sleep and I'll drive all the way. We should be home in about six hours."

"Yeah, I'm ready." She rubbed my leg. "Thank you, I love you so much."

I pulled her in and squeezed her body. "I love you, too."

CHAPTER 15

Claire

I remember little about the drive home. I was exhausted and must have fallen asleep straight away. It wasn't until the truck came to a stop and the silence of the motor woke me up. I rubbed my eyes and looked out of the window and recognized the carport of our home. "We're home already?" I asked in a sleepy voice.

"You've been asleep for hours and yes, we're home." Travis rubbed my shoulder. "Come on, let's get you into bed. I called my mom on the road and told her we were coming home early so she doesn't think we're intruders," Travis chuckled.

"Did she ask why we cut our trip short?"

"She did, and I told her you weren't feeling well, which is kind of true, you were sick."

Feeling emotionally drained, I gave him a weak smile. "Thanks.

Hopefully, she's asleep, I don't feel like talking to anyone right now. I just want to crawl into bed and fall asleep in your arms."

Travis squeezed my hand. "Come on. I'll unpack the truck in the morning."

To my relief, our place was dark. Caroline was sleeping, and Travis quickly grabbed Tilly, who jumped off the couch as soon as he opened the door.

"Shh Tilly, it's just mommy and daddy," he whispered, covering her snout to prevent her from barking.

I took Tilly from Travis' arms and held her tight while she licked my face ravenously. "Hey, girl, I've missed you," I whispered, as I carried her into the bedroom and placed her on our bed. Within minutes we were both under the covers with Tilly asleep settled in her favorite spot, on my pillow above my head.

Images of Davin haunted my sleep, and I woke to Travis calling my name in the early hours of the morning. "I want these night-mares to stop," I cried as he cradled me in his arms.

"Give it some time. Now that you know the truth about Davin, you can heal. Talking about it will help too, and I will always be here to help you do that."

I squeezed his hand that was resting on my chest. "I know that, and I love you for it." Tilly was sitting by the door while I looked over at it. "Hey, can you let Tilly out? I need to take a shower."

"You don't want to go back to sleep? It's not even 5:00 yet."

I sat up and raked my hands through my hair. "Nah, I'm awake now, a shower will do me good." I paused and took a deep breath. "You know, I've been thinking about what you said when you woke me up from my nightmare. I understand so much more about myself now that I know what Davin did to me. We both know I never dated much until I met you, and I've always had issues trusting men, it all makes so much sense now. I need to move forward from this and allow myself to heal, as you said."

Travis grinned. "That's my girl," he said, patting my thigh. "Why don't you take a nice long shower and I'll go make us a big break-fast with mom after I've taken Tilly out."

I shook my head. "Oh no, I don't want any food."

Travis creased his brow. "What? You haven't eaten since yesterday afternoon, are you still feeling nauseous?"

I brushed off his concerns. "The thought of food just turns my stomach, I'll be fine. It's probably a 24-hour bug or something."

"Well, if it continues, I'm taking you to the doctor."

I pulled my tired body out of bed and smiled. "I said I'll be fine. Now go on, Tilly is waiting and I'm going to take a shower."

Feeling refreshed from my shower and with my head in a better place, I joined Caroline and Travis in the living room, where I found them chatting over their morning coffee. Caroline stood and welcomed me with a warm smile and a hug while Tilly danced at my feet.

"Claire, welcome home. Travis told me you weren't feeling well, are you doing any better?"

"I'm doing okay, I just have an upset stomach. Thank you so much for watching Tilly."

Caroline picked up Tilly and kissed her snout. "Oh, we've had so much fun together, she's splendid company."

I petted Tilly's head while she was still in Caroline's arms. "Yes, she is."

Travis took a sip of his coffee before speaking. "After I've unpacked the truck, what do you want to do today?"

I took a seat next to him and rested my hand on his knee. "If you don't mind, I'd like to call Slater and Sabela and see if they're home today. I think I should talk to them."

Caroline couldn't hide the concern in her voice. "Is everything okay? You're not backing out of the Children's home, are you?"

I shook my head, realizing what I had said would make her think that. "No, of course not. I just want to smooth some things out before we move forward."

Travis understood and smiled. "I'll call them right now, I'm sure they're up with the twins," he chuckled, reaching for his phone on the coffee table.

"Thanks," I replied, and left to get a glass of water from the kitchen.

When I returned, Travis was still on the phone and ended the call a few minutes later.

"What did they say?" I asked.

"We're going to their house at noon, Sabela will be there, too."

"Great, thank you. I'll help you unpack the truck," then looked over at Caroline. "I don't mean to exclude you Caroline, but once I've talked to Slater and Sabela, I'll feel better about filling you in. Will you be okay staying here with Tilly? We shouldn't be too long, then we can talk about Travis going to Seattle to help you pack." I gave her a reassuring smile and took her hand. "I'm so excited that you'll be living and working with us at *Open Arms*."

"I'll be fine. You're sure everything is, okay?" Caroline asked.

"Yes, it will be. This is just something I need to do."

CHAPTER 16

Claire

Sabela greeted us with a warm smile, Joy cradled in her arms sleeping. "Hey guys, come on in. Let me put Joy down and I'll bring a pot of coffee to the kitchen table," she grinned. "I have beer, too."

I matched her smile, even though my stomach churned violently. I wasn't sure if it was from the nausea I'd been feeling or from my nerves. "Thanks, Sabela. Do you mind if I just have water?"

"Coffee sounds good to me," Travis added.

Sabela closed the front door with her free hand while Travis and I took a seat at the table. "Slater will be down soon, he's on the phone in the office. Make yourselves at home while I put this little girl in her crib."

The room fell silent once Sabela had left. I sat nervously next to Travis, rubbing my sweaty palms beneath the table.

Travis stroked my shoulder. "Are you okay?" he asked.

I didn't answer and left the table to get a bottle of water from the fridge. After taking a large gulp, I finally spoke while leaning against the sink. "Why am I so damn nervous? Sabela and Slater are our friends."

"Do you know what you want to say to them? You haven't told me anything, maybe if we talk about it first before they join us it may help ease your nerves."

I shook my head. "No, if I think about it too much or try to rehearse it, I may chicken out. This is the best way." I gave him a weak smile. "Then we can put all of this behind us and concentrate on *Open Arms*."

The sudden sound of footsteps coming down the stairs silenced me, and I returned to the table and took Travis' hand.

Slater smiled when he reached the table. "Hey, good to see you, can I get you some coffee?"

I held up my bottle. "I have water, but Travis will take a cup."

Slater had his back to us while he poured himself and Travis some coffee. "You guys are back early from your honeymoon. Don't tell me yours took a turn too?" he chuckled.

To my relief, Sabela joined us before either of us could reply. "Okay, both girls are asleep, and Scottie is playing with Legos in his room. You have our full attention," she laughed "but I can't say for how long, I'm on the kids' schedule."

"So, what's this all about?" Slater asked, as he pulled out a chair for Sabela and took a seat next to her.

My hand remained locked with Travis' as I took a deep breath and said, "I owe you both a huge apology."

Slater and Sabela gave each other a puzzled stare before looking at me. "For what?" Slater asked.

With my other hand, I rubbed my stomach, which was now in knots. "We should have talked at the hospital after Slater had shot Davin, but instead I shut you out."

Slater shifted nervously in his seat and avoided my eyes; I sensed he thought I was here to express my anger at him for killing my brother. They remained silent, and I continued to speak. "I couldn't talk about it because I didn't know how to react, and I honestly wanted to tell you that you did the right thing Slater, but I couldn't." I turned and looked at Sabela. "What Davin did to you was wrong, but I had also lost a brother that day, and I felt I couldn't or shouldn't mourn for him in front of you, it seemed so wrong after what he put you through."

Sabela interrupted me. "Claire, please, you're only human..."

I shook my head as tears pooled in my eyes. "Sabela, let me finish. We're about to embark into a business together, a dream of Travis' and mine that you two made come true, and for that we will be forever grateful. But I don't want this business to start with secrets, which is why I want to lay everything on the table and be completely honest with you. We shared our wedding day, the good and the bad, and we should be able to talk about it and remember it without worrying if we're upsetting one another over what happened on what was our special day, today or even ten years from now."

Sabela nodded, "I agree."

"So do I," Slater added.

"When Travis and I left for our honeymoon, I was confused about my feelings and felt it may jeopardize our future with *Open Arms*, but all that has changed."

Sabela creased her brow. "It has? You're doing better now?"

"I will be, it'll just take some time."

"Claire, what do you mean?" Sabela asked. "Are you talking about getting over the loss of Davin? We're terribly sorry."

I shook my head and rubbed my brow. "Please don't apologize." Tears trickled down my cheeks, and I quickly wiped them away. "When I was a little girl, my brother Davin molested me."

Sabela gasped and raised her hand to her mouth. "What?"

"That bastard," Slater hissed.

Travis squeezed my hand. "You don't have to say any more, Claire."

I brushed him off. "Yes, I do, Travis." I paused and took a deep breath. "It's why we came home early from our honeymoon. I've been having nightmares about Davin, and apparently, when we were kids, our parents took us to The Sequoia National Park, where Travis and I stayed for a few days. The trip triggered all kinds of childhood memories. At first, they were happy memories of Davin being the protective brother, and I was missing him. But when we booked into the Inn for the night because I wasn't feeling well, I had horrible flashbacks of Davin crawling into bed with me, and he was naked."

Sabela gasped again. "Oh, Claire, I'm so sorry, are you sure it happened?"

I gave her a vigorous nod. "Oh yes, it definitely happened, and at that Inn, too. That's why I had flashbacks, he molested his baby sister. Sabela, he was a monster long before he met or hurt you, or those other girls." I turned and looked at Slater, "you did the right thing by killing him, and I hate him. I'm so sorry for what he did to you, Sabela." I took another deep breath and wiped away more tears. "I'm telling you this because I feel it's important that you know I hold absolutely no resentment for what happened to Davin. He deserved it, and I can honestly say I'm ashamed to call him my brother and will never forgive him for what he did." I forced a weak smile. "I'm ready to move on and put all of this behind me. It'll take some time, but Travis and the children that will come to *Open Arms* will help me heal."

Sabela reached across the table and took my hand. "Oh Claire, we love you, and *Open Arms* is going to be amazing, not just for the kids, but for all of us, we can't wait." Her mood suddenly turned somber. "I have one more thing to ask you though about Davin." She paused. "Does your mom know what Davin did to you?"

I shook my head. "I haven't spoken to her since our wedding."

"Don't you think you should?" Sabela asked, "I think she has a right to know."

"When I'm ready to talk to her it'll be the first thing I tell her. I'm still upset with my parents for visiting Davin in jail behind my back, and I'm trying to deal with everything the best I can, I'm just not ready to face her yet."

Sabela gave me a soft smile. "I understand," leaning back in her chair and resting her hand on Slater's knee. "Let's talk about *Open Arms*, it won't be long until you move in." She turned and looked at Travis, "when are you leaving for Seattle to help your mom move?"

"We were going to go this weekend, but seeing that we're back early from our honeymoon, we're driving up there the day after tomorrow."

"Fantastic!" Sabela cheered. "How exciting to have your mom live with you after all the time you've missed with each other."

"She's an incredible woman. I understand why she had to give me up, and I blame her for nothing. It just feels great to have her in my life now."

"How long do you think you'll be gone?" Slater asked.

"Only four days. That will give us enough time to rest and get ready for moving day, and then the barbecue the following weekend," Travis replied.

Sabela rubbed her hands together and grinned. "I can't wait. Just think, in less than two weeks, you'll be welcoming children into your home and giving them a second chance in life."

I took Travis' hand and smiled, "yes, they'll be our family."

CHAPTER 17

Travis

$\mathcal{I}$ had never felt prouder of Claire than I did while we were talking to Slater and Sabela. The strength she showed while coming to terms with what Davin had done as well as accepting it was undeniable. It took courage for her to confess to Sabela and be true to her feelings when it came to Davin. I'll stand by her and help her with whatever she needs to do to move forward. I saw her take not just a step today, but a giant leap when she was finally honest with herself and realized she could no longer have any feelings for Davin but hatred.

When we left Slater and Sabela's, I held her close in the truck as she rested her head on my shoulder.

"Do you think I did the right thing?" she asked, while we sat at a red light.

"Definitely. Don't you feel better? Like a weight has been lifted off your shoulders? You're no longer suppressing your feelings, and Slater and Sabela know exactly where you stand and how you feel about Davin."

"I do feel better that I told them, I don't feel like I'm hiding anything now." She rubbed my thigh and smiled. "Thank you for not stopping me and being there for me."

"Hey, you knew exactly what you needed to do, there was no way I was going to stop you. Now we can start planning for our new family."

Claire gave me a genuine smile and sat up, "I can't wait to see the smiles on the children's faces when they arrive." Her eyes suddenly turned wide, "we need to have a welcome party, what do you think?"

"That's a brilliant idea, why didn't we think of that before?"

"Well, so much has been going on. I can plan it while you're in Seattle with your mom, I'll have Sabela help me."

I laughed as she squeezed her hands together. "Oh, this will be so much fun," she squealed. "We'll invite everyone to the barbecue."

We came to another red light, I turned to Claire and stroked her cheek. "Things are only going to get better from here on out."

She smiled. "I think you're right. Now, let's go home and plan for your trip to Seattle."

"Only if you promise to eat something, you still haven't eaten all day."

"I promise. I feel much better, in fact, a bit hungry. Maybe it was all the crap I was dealing with over the past few days and feeling extremely nervous before speaking to Slater and Sabela that was making me sick."

I nodded. "I never thought of that, you're probably right."

～

Saying goodbye to Claire two days later was difficult. We've never been apart except for when I was in a coma in the hospital, but back then I never knew it.

"I'm going to miss you so much," I told her as I held her in my arms outside my truck, my mom sitting patiently on the passenger side.

"I'm going to miss you, too. Promise me you'll let your mom drive when you get tired."

"I promise. Are you sure you're going to be okay by yourself?"

Claire chuckled, "I won't be by myself, I have Tilly." She patted my chest. "This afternoon, Sabela is coming over and we're going to talk about the welcome party for the kids. I'll be fine."

We kissed passionately outside my truck. "I'll wrap this up as fast as I can because I hate being away from you, and I haven't even left yet. I'll call you every chance I get, and you do the same."

She kissed me back with the same passion. "I will. Now get out of here before I jump in the truck with you, I love you."

"I love you, too," I said, as I stepped into the truck and fired up the motor. I turned to my mom browsing on her phone. "Are you ready, mom?"

She smiled. "I sure am."

Claire remained in the carport as I backed the truck out of the parking space, and as we exited onto the street, I stretched my arm out of the window and waved, watching her through my rearview mirror.

"Are you sure Claire will be okay?" my mom asked, as I turned onto the main road.

"She told me she would be, so I have to believe her."

"I know, but after what you two told me about her brother and what he'd done it can't be easy for her."

"No, it's not mom, but Claire is a strong woman and she'll get through this with our help." I turned and looked at my mom, "we need to be there for Claire and help her all we can."

"And we will, Travis. I love her as much as I love you. You did well, Travis, and I'm proud to call you my son."

I never get tired of hearing her call me her son. "And I'm proud to call you my mom. Now the sooner we get to Seattle, the sooner we can pack up your things and bring you home, which is where you belong."

CHAPTER 18

Claire

It's been a long four days without Travis but thank God I've been keeping busy with Sabela planning the welcome party for the children. Jill also insisted on helping, which I'm grateful for, and insisted on being in charge of hiring entertainment for the kids and a bouncy house. Sabela's mom Charlotte volunteered to make a cake which left Sabela and I to organize the food. We also bought each child a special welcome gift.

"Are you getting excited?" Sabela asked as we sat at the table in my house finalizing the plans for the party. "Soon you'll welcome three children into your home, and three more the next day."

My cheeks flushed with excitement. "Yes, I can't believe this is happening." I suddenly had a terrifying thought, "what if they don't all get along?"

Sabela laughed. "They're kids. They/re bound to have fallouts or fight over a toy, but you and Travis will be there to guide them.

You'll instill family values and trust, something that's been missing from their lives."

Before Travis left we went over the children's files that would move into *Open Arms*. There will be six; three would arrive next Tuesday, a week after moving day, and the other three would arrive the next day, Wednesday. Jasmine, a young girl of color, is seven and the eldest. She's been in and out of homes since she was two because her parents were in jail for selling and using drugs and lost custody of her. That poor girl, I know Travis will be an enormous influence in her life. He'll be able to relate to her, having spent all his childhood in the system.

"Some of these kids have gone through hell. No child should go through some of the things these children have endured," Sabela said.

"I know, we wish we could help all of them. The two boys, Colin is three, and Matthew, who will be three in two months, were put up for adoption by young mothers when they were born and are still without a forever home, it's so sad."

"And what about the other three?" Sabela asked.

"They're all girls. Kate just turned four and has been in the system for two years. Parents were abusive. Then there's Nicole and Janet. Both are five and from drug and alcohol addicted parents who lost custody of them around four years ago." I paused and took a deep breath. "We're going to do everything we can to make these children feel welcome and trust us."

Sabela smiled. "I know you will, both your backgrounds ensure that. These six kids are incredibly lucky to have you come into their lives and give them a fresh start."

"It's nerve-wracking, we'll be instant parents to six children, and I don't want to mess it up."

"You won't, you and Travis have so much to give. I have all the faith in the world in the two of you."

I rubbed my sweaty palms together. "Thanks. Travis should be home later today," I grinned. "Thank God, I've missed him so much. Tomorrow we'll start packing, and Friday is the big moving day and barbecue."

"Yes," Sabela squealed. "Do you have a lot to pack?"

"No, most of our furniture is going to the Salvation Army. With the Children's home being completely furnished, we don't need it."

Sabela squealed again and clapped her hands. "Oh, this is so exciting. Slater is in charge of organizing the barbecue, and from what he's told me it's all under control. We're all planning on being at your house on Friday morning to help you, even my mom and Lorenzo are coming."

"Oh, that is so sweet of them, I love your mom."

Sabela hesitated before speaking. "Have you talked to your mom?"

I shook my head. "No, I'm not ready." I released a nervous laugh, "I'm not sure if I ever will be." I stood up hastily. "Listen, I should go, I want to be home when Travis gets back. I'll call you tomorrow."

"Are you okay? I'm sorry, I didn't mean to intrude regarding your mom."

"Yeah, I'm fine. I just don't know what to say when it comes to my mom. I gotta go," I said in a rush, grabbing my purse off the table and heading for the front door.

Once outside I sucked in some fresh air and marched to my car, feeling annoyed that my mother still angered me so much and still had such a negative impact on me.

When I arrived home, Tilly soon cheered me up with her wet kisses, dancing around my feet. I picked her up and cuddled with her on the couch. "Daddy is coming home today. Have you missed him as much as I have?" I petted the top of her head before standing. "Come on, let's get you a biscuit." Tilly knew the word and instantly barked with excitement as I headed towards the kitchen. I stopped halfway and closed my eyes as I rubbed my brow. "Oh wow! I just got really dizzy, I must have stood up too fast," I said out loud, as I continued to rub my head and tried to open my eyes, but the room was spinning. "Oh man, I suddenly don't feel so good." Afraid I might fall, I grabbed onto the back of the chair and remained still, hoping the dizziness would soon pass. After a few minutes, my head continued to spin. "Tilly, I must lie down for a bit. Why don't you come and join me? Mama is not feeling too good."

CHAPTER 19

Travis

Spending the last four days with my mom has been incredible, and although we talked about everything there was to talk about while she'd been staying with us, we talked for hours on the drive to Seattle. I told her more about my childhood memories, making sure I didn't make her feel guilty about anything I shared with her. I only shared fond memories, which were few.

When we pulled into the apartment building where she lived, it was exactly how she'd described it. "My place is small and plain compared to where you and Claire live, I don't live in a fancy condo," she said.

I reassured her, "it's fine mom, I don't judge you by where you live, I love you for you."

"Well, it's all I can afford," she confirmed. "I'm just a little embarrassed."

"Well, in a short time you'll be living in a mansion with your son and daughter-in-law and taking care of six children that need us."

"I know, it still feels like a dream, Travis. The house is beautiful, you and Claire have done an amazing job getting it ready, I'm so proud of you."

Kids were playing football in the parking lot at the rear of the building. As we drove by, they stepped aside to let us through. I couldn't help but notice their torn jeans and stained shirts and assumed they were hand-me-downs or thrift store bargains.

When I stepped out of the truck, I could hear loud music from an upstairs apartment and shouting from another. "Are they okay?" I asked my mom. "The woman sounds pretty pissed off."

"Yeah, her husband probably came home drunk again. They argue all the time, day and night, god knows when they sleep."

I followed my mum to a flight of stairs at the side of the building and waved flies away from my face. As we walked by the open dumpster, I gasped when I saw a rat run underneath it, "shit, I just saw a rat."

"Won't be the first," my mom noted as we climbed the stairs.

Even though I admire my mom for turning her life around and getting sober, I couldn't deny that I was glad she was coming to live with us and getting out of this place.

My mom's apartment was a small one-bedroom, very dark with the drapes closed. "Let me get some light in here," she said, pulling the drapes open. "I keep them closed when I'm not home."

I glanced around the small room where we stood and noticed a small kitchen with a counter at the other end of the room. One wall of the living room had wall-to-wall bookshelves with no space for any more books. "You like to read, mom?"

"Yes, I read every night in bed. These books saved me when I was getting my act together, they were my escape," she chuckled. "Still are."

"That's a lot of books mom, I'm not sure if we can take them all." I scanned the room. "How much of this furniture do you want to take? Your room at our house will have all new furniture."

"I'm leaving most of it behind. The landlord will be pleased, he'll leave it here and charge more rent because the place will be furnished, I'm only taking the small stuff."

I pointed to a door off to the right, "is that the bedroom?"

My mom nodded. "Yes, go ahead and check it out. I'll be leaving the bed and dressers, but I'm taking all my clothes and stuff."

I walked over to the door and pushed it open. It was a small room, just like the others, and dark because of the closed drapes. My mom, close behind me pulled them open, and the first thing I noticed was a picture on the nightstand. It was a photo of a baby, and I picked it up to get a closer look. My mom stood next to me and brushed her hand across the frame, "that's you, Travis."

My jaw dropped. "That's me?"

"Yes. It's the only picture I have of you. You were just a few hours old. Every night for the past 30 years I've looked at that picture and kissed you goodnight. Not a day has gone by that I didn't think of you and wonder where you were and what you were doing with your life."

"How did you get a picture of me? You didn't have cell phones back then?"

"There was a really sweet nurse at the hospital where I had you. I still remember her name, Judith. I was forced to give you up, and she was young, she listened to me shortly after you were born and held me in her arms as I cried my eyes out. She asked me if I would like a picture of you, and of course I said yes. The next morning, she brought her camera to work and took that picture of you. We met two weeks later during her lunch break and she gave me the picture, but made me promise not to show it to anyone or tell anyone where I got it from because it could cost her her job."

"Do you still keep in touch with her?"

My mom shook her head. "No, that was also something we agreed to, to not keep in touch. She couldn't risk losing her job if someone ever found out about the photo. If we had remained friends, it could lead back to her."

Over the next two days as we packed, I saw another side of my mom. I lived her life for those few days, along with the couple of rats that I saw race across the living room floor and under the couch. She shared photos of herself as a child, as well as a few that she had of her mother and father. I could finally put a face to my grandparents whom I'd wondered about so many times in my life.

She was ready to leave it all behind to begin her new life with her son and make up for lost time. We stood together in the now bare living room, my arm draped over her shoulder. "Are you ready mom? We have a long drive ahead of us."

My mom reached up and squeezed my hand, "yes, I am, I don't think I'll be missing this place too much."

Twenty hours later, making few stops and taking turns driving we pulled into the carport of the condo. The silence of the motor was welcoming, which woke my mom up, who'd been sleeping for the past few hours. I checked the time on my phone and was pleased to see we'd made it back at a reasonable hour. It was close to 5:00 PM, giving me some quality time to spend with Claire. I couldn't wait to see her and ushered my mom out of the truck. "Come on mom, let's go, I'll unpack the truck tomorrow."

I heard Tilly barking on the other side of the door when I inserted my key into the lock and opened the door. "Hey girl," I said, as I knelt to pet her. "Claire! We're home," I called, Tilly at my feet. There was no answer which concerned me. My mom closed the door behind me.

"Claire?" I called again.

"Maybe she stepped out," my mom suggested.

"Her car is in the carport, if she went for a walk, she would have taken Tilly."

"I called her name again as I walked toward the bedroom where I found the door open, "Claire, are you in here?"

I stopped at the doorway when I spotted her sleeping. I turned and looked at my mom petting Tilly. "She's sleeping, it's not like her to sleep during the day."

"Wake her up, make sure she's okay," my mom ordered.

"I hate to wake her, but you're right, I'll be right back."

I tiptoed to the bed and chuckled when I heard her faint snore. Mesmerized by her beauty with her head resting on the pillow and her hand gently resting on her cheek, I stood still for a moment to admire my beautiful wife. "I'm home, baby," I whispered, as I quietly sat next to her on the bed and stroked her cheek. "Hey, beautiful, I'm home."

She stirred and slowly opened her eyes and smiled when her eyes met mine. "Travis, you're home," she said, holding out her arms.

I leaned in and held her tight. "I've missed you so much," she said in a sleepy voice.

I stroked her back. "I've missed you, too, are you feeling okay? Why are you sleeping in the middle of the afternoon?"

Claire pulled herself up to a sitting position and rubbed her eyes again. "I felt dizzy, and I came in here to lie down for a bit. What time is it?"

"A little after five."

"Oh wow, I've been asleep for a few hours."

"What do you mean, you felt dizzy? Did you faint?" I asked.

"No, but I felt like I was going to which is why I came in here."

"I'm taking you to the doctor tomorrow. You were sick last week and today you almost fainted."

Claire rolled her eyes. "I'm fine, I don't need to see a doctor."

I gave her a smirk. "Remember when you bossed me around after I got home from the hospital and insisted I do things for my recovery? Well wifey, it's my turn now, and I'm not taking no for an answer, I'm calling the doctor in the morning."

CHAPTER 20

Claire

Travis had a point; I was strict with him when he was recovering from the coma. I raised my hands in defeat, "okay, okay, I'll go to the doctor if it's tomorrow, there's no time after that. The day after, everyone will be here to help us finish packing and move, then there's the barbecue."

"I'll make sure I get you an appointment tomorrow, I'll call first thing in the morning, then my mom and I are taking her things over to the new house so we can have an empty truck for our stuff."

"Sounds good. I can stay here and do some more packing." I stretched and released a yawn, "I'm feeling much better, so I'm going to get up and get something to eat. Do you want anything?"

Travis raised his hands to stop me from leaving the room, "oh no you don't, you're going to take it easy, I'll fix you something."

"You will do no such thing, you and Caroline have been driving for the past twenty hours. I'll put some chicken on and make us all a salad, you two must be starving."

Travis didn't object and allowed me to make dinner for all of us.

"So, it's official Caroline, you are no longer a resident of Seattle. How do you feel? Are you going to miss your old place?" I asked her.

Caroline cracked a laugh. "Oh, good lord no. You'll never have the privilege of seeing that dump but Travis did, and I'm sure he'll tell you all about it someday."

"Oh come on mom, it wasn't that bad."

"Travis, you're being too kind, you freaked out when you saw the rats."

My jaw dropped. "You had rats? Oh my god, well that says enough right there, I don't think you'll be missing that place."

After dinner, Travis leaned back in his chair and smiled at me. "Do you want to call it an early night? That long drive is catching up with me and besides, I haven't seen you in four days, I want to crawl into bed and hold you in my arms."

I matched his smile, "that sounds good, I'd love that."

Travis turned to his mom, "do you mind, mom?"

Caroline gave him the okay with a quick wave. "You two lovebirds go right ahead, I'm tired too. I'm going to go to bed and read for a while, mind if I take Tilly? I've missed the little girl."

"Sure mom, we'll see you in the morning," Travis said.

Caroline stood and called Tilly from the couch. "Goodnight, see you both tomorrow."

I woke up the next morning the same way I'd fallen asleep, wrapped in Travis' arms with my head resting on his bare chest. The sound of his snores told me he was sound asleep. I gently lifted his arm from around my neck and placed it on his chest. He stirred for a moment and then rolled onto his side with his back facing me. Feeling relieved he hadn't woken up, I inched my way out of bed and quickened my pace once my feet were firmly on the carpet and left the room.

It surprised me to see Caroline already up drinking coffee while Tilly slept on her lap. "Caroline, you're up early, I thought you'd be sleeping in after your long trip yesterday."

Caroline turned her head to face me, "I couldn't sleep."

"Are you okay? Is something on your mind?"

"Well, now that this is all happening and I've given up my apartment in Seattle, the reality of it all is somewhat scary."

I took a seat next to her and Tilly immediately stirred and moved onto my lap." What do you mean? I hope you're not having second thoughts; we really need you at *Open Arms*, and the idea of the three of us working and living together is amazing."

"Oh I hope so, Claire. I just hope it doesn't destroy what rela-tionship Travis and I have built over these past few weeks. I've heard such terrible and sad stories of mother and child working and living under the same roof, and then end up hating each other. It happened to my neighbor in Seattle who worked with her son for three years in a restaurant they'd started together, and they also bought a house. She lost everything, her share of the restau-rant and the house, and had to start over with nothing, ending up in the building where I lived. She now works at Walmart, barely making ends meet. I don't want anything to happen between Travis and I, he just came back into my life and I couldn't bear to lose him again."

I rested my hand on her shoulder, "Caroline, Travis loves you very much, he feels complete now that you're in his life. Just like you, it would devastate him if he lost you again, you'll be fine, please don't worry, okay?"

"Okay, I'll try not to." She paused for a few seconds and then spoke again. "Claire, can I share something with you? I feel it would be uncomfortable to share with Travis because I gave him up."

"Sure, what is it?"

"The closer it gets to the children arriving the more anxious I'm feeling, but I also have this rush of excitement when I think about it."

I wasn't sure what she was getting at and gave her my best reply, "I can understand that and I think we're all pretty excited."

"Yes I know we are, but I've never been around children. I missed out completely when it came to raising kids, and there's always been this void in my life." She smiled and took my hand, "I can see this home filling some of that void. Not all of it, because I'll never get back what I missed with Travis, but being around children, and helping you and Travis raise them and guide them will be so rewarding, it brings tears to my eyes. I can't thank you both enough for giving me this chance."

My eyes teared up as Caroline confessed her feelings. "Oh, Caroline, that's beautiful, it seems like you need the children as much as they need you."

She nodded, "Yes, I believe so." She squeezed my hand, "please don't tell Travis, it's hard to explain to the child I gave up."

I understood her uneasiness. "I won't, I promise, that's something you should tell him if you ever decide to."

"Thank you, I appreciate that."

The bedroom door opened, interrupting us, and Travis appeared wearing grey sweats and a white T-shirt. "Morning, ladies," he said, followed by a yawn. "Is there any coffee?"

"Yes, I made a pot about an hour ago," Caroline replied, before standing. "What time do you want to leave, Travis?" she asked.

"In about an hour, I need to make an appointment for Claire at the doctor's before we leave."

Caroline turned to me, "is everything okay?"

I smiled, "yes, I'm fine." I turned my attention to Travis, "honey, I'm feeling great, there's no need to call the doctor."

Travis raised his hand in protest, "remember what I said last night, how I did everything you asked when I was sick? Now you're going to listen to me young lady, and we're going to see the doctor today if I can get you in."

"Why do you need to see the doctor, Claire?" Caroline asked.

"Ask your son," I joked. "I had an upset stomach the other day, and yesterday I got dizzy, now Travis is insisting I get checked out."

"Well I'm sorry Claire, but I have to agree with Travis, you should get checked out, you can never be too careful nowadays. A little something can turn into something serious."

Travis clapped his hands. "Thank you, mom! See wifey, it's two against one, you lose. I'm calling the doctor."

I leaned back on the couch and folded my arms before giving them a smirk, "fine, I'll go."

CHAPTER 21

Travis

I got Claire an appointment with the doctor at 1:00 PM, giving my mom and I enough time to unload her stuff at *Open Arms*. It pleased me Slater was there making final preparations for tomorrow's moving day barbecue.

When I stepped out of the truck onto the driveway, little Scottie left his father's side from inside the garage and raced toward me.

"Uncle Travis!" he screamed as he ran into my arms.

"Hey buddy, are you helping your dad?"

"I sure am," he replied in a proud voice.

"Hey man," Slater hollered from the garage, "give me a sec, I'm on a call."

I waved my hand. "Sure, no problem. We're going to take my mom's things up to her room."

"I'll give you a hand when I'm done here," Slater replied, holding his phone away from his ear.

I turned to Scottie who was talking to my mom, "hey Scottie, do you want to help?"

"Can I?" he said, with wide eyes.

I handed him a small, light box. "Why don't you follow Caroline with this?"

Beaming with pride, Scottie took the box and marched next to my mom into the house through the grand double-door entrance. I still couldn't believe this was going to be our home. It was a beautiful seven-bedroom, five-bath mansion we had spent so much time remodeling and making perfect for the children that were about to become part of our family.

I grabbed a box from the bed of the truck and walked inside. Claire had done a fantastic job picking out the colors for the place, the grand foyer was lined with a wooden coat rack that included a bench and a bin with each child's name painted on the front which Claire designed and I made. The walls were a light pastel blue, and we kept the elegant chandelier because Claire loved how it sparkled and made patterns on the walls.

Off to the left was a spacious room with a giant flat screen, a play area for the kids, colorful bean bags, and a giant, wrap-around couch where we could all cuddle on for family movie night. While I was admiring our work and our new home Slater entered the house. "Looks great, doesn't it?" I said.

"It sure does with Claire's touch." Slater headed towards the kitchen, "do you want a beer? I just filled the fridge."

"Sure," I said, as I followed him past the dining room and took a seat at the counter. We did not have to do much in the kitchen, Eve, the previous owner who sadly passed away, had good taste, and all the stainless-steel appliances were brand new when Slater took ownership. The only major addition Claire had added was a chore list and an awards chart, which I thought was a brilliant idea. She used blackboard paint and painted one entire wall with it and designed the chart so that it was easy for the kids to read and write on. Another fabulous idea by wifey.

The bright living room, off from the kitchen with its many large windows which overlooked the ocean and the double doors that led out to the large deck, was now a learning room. We'd decided to homeschool the older kids until they'd had time to adjust and bring the younger ones in here too, for crafts and reading. Claire and I spent many weeks interviewing private tutors, and after long, nightly discussions together, we went over their qualifications, personalities and experiences, and both agreed that Helen Hash would be perfect for the position and would start a week after the children had arrived.

Slater joined me at the counter that separated the two rooms and took a seat, "here you go," he said, handing me a beer.

"Thanks."

Slater took a swig of his drink, "so I've told everyone to be at your place at 10:00 AM tomorrow. Four of us have trucks, so we should have you all moved in here in no time, and everyone is bringing food for the barbecue afterward. Sabela's mom and Lorenzo will come to your house too, and they'll gather everyone's food from their vehicles and bring it here."

"That's a great idea."

I suddenly felt a tug on my T-shirt and turned to see Scottie standing at my side. "Hey, buddy."

He smiled. "Do you have more stuff for me to carry? I want to help."

I chuckled at his cuteness. "Sure, let's go out to the truck and see what we can find," I said, as I stood and gave Slater a nod. "We should be helping, not sitting here drinking beer," I laughed.

Slater took another swig, "you're right." He smiled at his son and held out his hand, "come on big guy, let's go."

At the truck Slater handed Scottie another light box, then we grabbed whatever we could carry in one trip. Upstairs, I found my mom in her room, hanging clothes in the closet.

"It's looking great in here, mom."

"I love it, it's so bright with the large windows and French doors that look out onto the ocean." The doors were open, and the light white curtains blew gently from the ocean breeze. "I can smell the ocean. It's going to be glorious to wake up here every morning." She took my hand and led me out onto the small deck, "look at this view, I'll be having coffee and reading a book here every morning."

"I'm sure you will, mom. Let me grab some more stuff and I'll be right back."

When I left my mom's room, I stood on the landing and admired the wooden signs Claire had put on each bedroom door with the children's names. Nicole and Janet would share a room, Colin and Matthew in another, and Jasmine, the eldest, would share with Kate. Off to the left was my mom's office, and at the end of the hallway was the master bedroom, which was ours.

It was all coming together. In a short time amongst these walls, the pitter patter of children's feet running up and down the stairs would fill this house, along with the laughter of children.

Open Arms was about to be born.

CHAPTER 22

Claire

While Travis was helping his mom, I spent the morning taking Tilly for a walk and packing the rest of our things. Unsure of what was going on with the condo full of boxes, Tilly kept close to my side and wouldn't let me out of her sight.

"It's okay girl, we're going to a new home where you will have a big green lawn to play on and kids to play ball with," I laughed. "You're going to be so tuckered out every night from running around all day and playing with the kids, you'll probably sleep all night, and oh what a blessing that'll be. Better yet, daddy has put in two doggie doors for you and that means no more taking you out to go to the bathroom." I petted her snout, "you can go out whenever you want to, I'm not sure who's more pleased, Travis and I or you."

Tilly barked like she understood me, running circles around

my feet. From the bedroom I heard the front door open and Travis' voice.

"Hey Claire, we're back."

I called from the bedroom where I was packing the last of our clothes, "in here, how did it go?"

I heard Travis walk through the living room and into the bedroom, "great, Mom is all unpacked and is going to watch Tilly while we go to the doctor, we have to leave here in fifteen minutes."

"You know, I'm feeling much better today, I feel stupid going when I'm feeling good. We can call and cancel if you'd like?"

Travis shook his head and waved his hand at me, "oh no you don't, I want to get you checked out; the fact that you almost fainted worries me."

I rolled my eyes, "I probably just got up too fast."

"Well, I'd feel better when the doctor confirms that."

I knew I was defeated and packed the last pair of jeans in the box. "Fine, let me go freshen up."

"Boy, you can be stubborn when you want to be. I'll be in the front room."

I had to admit that his concerns touched me, but I was certain that I'd gotten a stomach virus on our trip and got dizzy from standing up too fast. In less than ten minutes I was ready to go and grabbed a light sweater in case an afternoon breeze picked up.

"Okay, I'm ready," I called to Travis, who was sitting on the couch browsing his phone. Travis stood and called his mom who was still in her room, "we're leaving, mom. Tilly's out here on the couch."

Caroline's door opened and she peeked her head out, "okay, I'm getting changed. I'll leave the door open so she can come in when she wakes up."

"I still think this is unnecessary," I said, climbing into Travis' truck. "We have too much to do, we're moving tomorrow."

Travis released a sarcastic laugh. "Will you stop? You've lost this one, now buckle up."

Because of the heavy traffic which is nothing new in these parts, we made it to the doctor's office with just minutes to spare. After putting the truck in park and turning off the motor, Travis jumped out and ushered me out.

"Come on wifey, let's go."

"I'm coming," I stated, as I trotted around the truck and took his hand. "I don't know what the rush is, we'll be sitting in the waiting room for at least an hour like we always do."

As I sat in my seat, shifting around for the next 40 minutes in the waiting room, I said "see, I told you we'd be waiting forever. What's the point of having an appointment if they don't keep to the time?"

"They should call us soon, they've probably been busy and got set back," Travis replied.

"This happens every time, don't these people realize we have a life?" I complained.

Travis rubbed my knee. "Hey, calm down, it's not like you to get so moody."

I leaned back in my chair and rubbed my brow. "I'm sorry. It's just that there's so much to do at home, and this just feels like a waste of time."

The sound of my name being called interrupted my rant, and I looked over at the door leading to the doctor's office and saw a young nurse looking our way.

I waved, "that's me," and quickly stood. "Come on, let's go," I told Travis.

The nurse led us through an array of corridors to a room with an examination table and two chairs.

"Please have a seat," the nurse requested, bringing up my file on the nearby computer. "What brings you here today, Claire?"

"Well, it was my husband that insisted I come. I'm feeling fine now, but last week I had an upset stomach and nausea for a couple of days, and the other day I had a dizzy spell and almost fainted."

The nurse smiled." Your husband is right, you should get checked out."

After asking me basic questions about my health and taking my weight and blood pressure, she entered the info into the computer. "The doctor will be along shortly."

I gave her a courteous smile, "thanks."

The doctor entered the room ten minutes later and I immediately sat up straight.

He stood in front of the computer monitor and scrolled through my file. "You've not been well, Claire?" he asked.

"I'm fine now, but not so great for the past few days."

"Well, all your vitals look fine. I'd like to do some blood tests and see if they'll tell us anything. If everything comes back fine, then it would appear you had some sort of short-span virus."

I nudged Travis' elbow. "See, I told you."

Travis smirked. "We don't have the results yet." He turned and looked at the doctor, "how long does it take to get the results back?"

"Just a couple of days. my office will call you. The blood nurse will be in shortly to take your blood."

"Great," I said hastily. "Thank you, doctor."

After the doctor left I leaned back in my chair and rested my head against the wall. "I hope we don't have to wait too long for the blood nurse."

Travis chuckled, "you're impossible, worse than a kid. Was I this bad when you took care of me?"

"No, you were much worse, I had to drag you to the doctor and to therapy."

A few minutes later there was a knock at the door and another nurse entered the room, wheeling in her bloodwork cart.

It took less than five minutes to have my blood drawn, and as soon as the nurse left I quickly stood, "okay we're all done here, let's go."

Travis laughed and shook his head. "I'm coming."

CHAPTER 23

Claire

The sound of Travis' cheerful voice woke me. "Wake up, wifey, it's moving day."

I felt his warm breath on my cheek and then a gentle kiss. "Come on sleeping beauty, it's time to get up, everyone's going to be here in a few hours."

Still half asleep, I rolled over to face him and smiled, "what time is it?"

"6:30," Travis said with a big grin before smacking me and tickling my sides vigorously. I quickly brought my knees up to my chest and screamed "stop! That tickles!"

He laughed and tickled me one more time, followed by a roar and a loud laugh. "I'll keep tickling you as long as you lie in bed."

I playfully pushed him away. "Okay, okay, I'm getting up, but you have to get off me first."

Travis leaned in and planted a kiss on my lips before rolling off my body and standing. I shook my head and sat up, "man, if it's not Tilly waking me up it's you, who needs an alarm clock?" I laughed, swinging my legs over the side of the bed and standing up. "I'm going to jump in the shower, can you put the coffee on and see where Tilly is? She may need to go out." I released a big smile, "this is the last day we need to let her out morning, noon and night. Starting tomorrow she'll be independent; I think I'm going to like that."

Travis pulled on some sweats and a T-shirt. "I hear my mom in the kitchen, she probably has the coffee on already, I'll go check."

When I stepped out of the shower I heard voices coming from the front room. They weren't Travis' or Caroline's, "who's here already? It's only a little past seven in the morning," I mumbled to myself.

I quickly dressed in jeans and a tank top and opened the bedroom door and saw Logan and Sadie standing in the front room talking to Travis.

I raked my hands through my damp hair and smiled when they looked my way. "Hey, guys, you're here bright and early."

"Yeah, I hope that's okay. Logan went for a morning surf, and I hung out at the beach to watch, it gives me such a rush," she giggled. "When he was done we didn't want to drive across town, so I figured we'd just come right over here."

I waved my hand and shook my head. "Oh, it's fine, you don't surf?" I asked Sadie.

Sadie tossed back her head and laughed, "oh god no, Logan plans on teaching me in the future, but I keep telling him it won't happen unless I overcome my fear of the ocean."

Her confession surprised me. "Really? You don't like the water? So, I guess swimming is out of the question?"

Sadie shook her head again, "oh hell no, you won't catch me in the water. I don't know what it is but I'm deathly afraid of being knocked down by a wave and getting sucked under."

"Wow, sorry to hear that." I quickly changed the subject, not sure how to respond. "Hey, I was about to get some coffee, would like some?"

Both nodded at the same time. "That'd be great, thanks," Logan replied, bending down to pet Tilly.

Sadie and I left the two men chatting in the front room and headed for the kitchen where Caroline was loading up the dishwasher.

I tapped her on the shoulder, "I can get those, why don't you go sit down and drink your coffee?"

Caroline waved me off. "I've got this, I wanted to clean the last of these dishes so I can pack them up before the rest of your friends arrive."

Sadie scanned the small kitchen, "this is a cute little place."

I smiled. "Yeah, it's served its purpose for a few years, now we're onto better things," I said, grabbing two cups out of the dishwasher.

"Claire!" Caroline yelled jokingly, "I'm trying to clean the dishes, not dirty them."

"Well, we only left out four, and Sadie and Logan want a cup."

Caroline shook her head as she closed the dishwasher door and started the machine. "I told you we should have gotten paper plates and cups, these dishes would have been packed by now."

"I know, but I've had no chance to stop at the store."

By 8:30, everyone had arrived, and suddenly my condo seemed much smaller, I don't think it's ever seen so many people at one time. Sabela's mom, Charlotte and her boyfriend Lorenzo had arrived first and immediately started to take things out of my fridge that I'd pointed out to her were for the party. Jill and Ricky arrived soon after along with Slater and Sabela. Little Scottie bounced around the condo like the energizer bunny until Charlotte cornered him and asked him to help her gather everyone's food that they'd brought for the barbecue. Scottie enthusiastically did one last jump and followed Charlotte around the condo as she told everyone to meet her and Lorenzo in the parking lot to give them the food they'd prepared and put it in their car.

After everyone had gathered around the twins, Joy and Hope,

who sat in their car seats, and admired their cuteness, and gave them baby kisses and hugs, Charlotte and Lorenzo took them down to their car to take them to *Open Arms*.

It didn't take long to load up their car. After they'd left to head over to *Open Arms* the rest of us gathered back at the condo.

Jill scanned the living room where we all stood as Ricky played tag with Scottie around the room. "Man, you guys have been busy," she said, pointing to the pile of boxes against the wall. "All that stuff is going?"

I nodded, "yep, and each room has more boxes. All the furniture is going to the Salvation Army, except for a few sentimental things that I've marked. They'll be here at noon so we have to make sure they'll have parking."

Sabela raised her hand, "Slater and I brought both our trucks over, and we're parked on the street right outside the building. We can move when they get here, then they can take our spots."

"Perfect. We'll go out there ten minutes before they arrive and wait for them, then shuffle the vehicles," I smiled. "Thanks, that was easy."

After finishing a conversation with Travis, Slater took the lead, raising his voice and arms to be heard above the chatter. "Okay, listen up everyone, me and the guys will take the heavy boxes and leave the lighter ones for you ladies."

Suddenly panic raced through me, and I screamed, "where's Tilly? The front door is open!" The room fell silent from my scream and I yelled her name, "Tilly!"

The room echoed her name as everyone split up and called her name again. We raced from room to room to hunt for her.

"Tilly baby, where are you? Come to mama," I cried, tears welling up in my eyes. "Come on Tilly."

Travis met me in the kitchen where I was checking all the cupboards. "Any luck?"

I shook my head in despair. "No, she's not here."

"Fuck!" Travis hissed under his breath as he made his way towards me and took me in his arms. "Don't worry, we'll find her."

"She's not here Travis, we've looked everywhere."

"She has to be, maybe she's sleeping."

I pulled away from his embrace. "Where else is there?" I barked, heading back to the front room where I found Jill and Ricky searching under the couch as Slater and Sabela checked the bedrooms with Caroline.

"Any luck, Jill?"

She looked over with sad eyes, "no, I'm afraid not."

"Who the fuck left the front door open, and where are Logan and Sadie?"

"They're checking the hallway," Ricky replied.

"Do you know who left the door open?" I asked again.

Jill slowly raised her head, her cheeks flushed with guilt.

I gave her a hard stare, "it was you, Jill?"

Jill avoided eye contact with me and stared at the floor. "I'm sorry, I went and propped opened the main entrance door to the building so it would be easier to carry the boxes out, I forgot about Tilly."

My body stiffened when I heard her, and I clenched my fist tightly against my body so I wouldn't reach out and smack her. "How can you be so stupid, Jill? You of all people who has a dog, how could you forget about Tilly?" Suddenly I froze and my eyes grew wide with a terrifying thought, "wait, you opened the main door at the end of the hallway?"

Jill nodded in shame.

"Is it still open?"

"I don't know, Sadie and Logan went out there," Jill replied.

"God damn it Jill, what the hell were you thinking?" I screamed, racing to the front door that was now closed, pulling it open with force.

"Tilly!" I screamed, racing down the hallway. My body shook

with fear when I saw there was no sign of her. "Come on, Tilly, where are you, baby?"

To my dismay, the main door to the building was propped open with a rock. I shook my head, "fucking Jill," I hissed.

I heard footsteps behind me and turned around; Slater and Sabela were racing towards me. "I have a terrible feeling she went outside," I cried as they approached me.

Slater held my trembling body. "We're going to find her. Jill, Ricky, and Caroline are going to keep looking around the condo. We left Scottie with them, too, I don't want him running around near the roads." He turned his head, "here comes Travis."

Travis handed me my cell phone, "here, make sure you always carry this, Tilly's collar has your number on it. Someone may find her and call you."

"Good idea," I said, sniffing back my tears as I put it in the back pocket of my jeans.

We all called Tilly's name as we walked outside and saw Logan and Sadie combing the sidewalk calling Tilly and searching the flower beds and bushes.

"Tilly!" I called as loud as I could. "Where the hell is she? She's never gotten out before, she wouldn't have any idea where to go."

My fear was rising, and I was terrified I'd never find her. I fell into Travis' arms, "I can't lose her, we have to find her."

Travis pulled me in close and rubbed my shoulder. "We will."

CHAPTER 24

Travis

I felt so helpless and scared but I tried to hold it together for Claire, I wasn't about to give up. The thought that we may not find Tilly terrified the hell out of me, Tilly and I bonded the day I moved in with Claire. I cringed as a car raced by and I yelled at the driver, "slow the fuck down," fearing Tilly could have been on the road. The driver responded by sticking his middle finger out the window.

"Asshole," I yelled, as he raced around the corner.

"Travis, that's not going to help," Claire said, checking the bush next to where she was standing.

"I know, but what if Tilly was on the road the moment he came speeding by?"

"I don't want to think about that. Come on, let's comb every inch of this side of the street and then walk back on the other side."

With space between us we all walked to the next block, calling her name repeatedly, with Sadie and Logan walking ahead of us. Our eyes were peeled, looking at the ground and on the porches, steps and bushes around us.

By the time we reached the other side of the street across from our building, there was still no sign of Tilly and we were thinking the worst - that we may never find her. I couldn't let that happen, there was no way we could just abandon the search and continue with our day. Barbecuing and partying with friends was the last thing on my mind. How are we even able to move from this neighborhood knowing Tilly is out there somewhere and possibly hurt? I didn't want to think of the other possibility and quickly erased it from my mind.

We stood in a group, all eyes scanning the surroundings as we spoke.

"I don't know where else to look," Sadie said. "I don't know this neighborhood very well."

"She's so tiny, she can't have gotten that far," Claire stated, desperation in her voice.

"If you were Tilly, where would you go?" I asked Claire.

Claire was silent for a moment as she put herself in Tilly's head, then suddenly gasped, hope in her voice. "The park, I would go to the park!" Her voice raised in excitement, "she loves it there."

"How far is the park from here?" Slater asked.

"A few blocks," I replied.

Slater looked over at Logan and Sadie, "why don't you two continue to look near Claire and Travis' building, and Sabela and I will go to the park with Travis and Claire."

Everyone nodded in agreement before we split up as Slater and Sabela followed us to the park. I had a hard time keeping up with Claire who was practically running ahead of me calling her name, "Tilly!" she yelled.

When we reached the entrance to the park, we split up. "You take the north side," I told Slater and Sabela, "we'll take the south side." I pointed to our regular bench next to the grand oak tree where we would sit with Tilly on our walks and watch her play with her ball. "We'll meet you back here at that bench."

Ten minutes into our search there was still no sign of Tilly; I was getting very worried and scared, I couldn't imagine life without her. The sadness in Claire's eyes was heart-wrenching. I held her close, my arms wrapped around her waist as we continued our search, calling her name and stopping anyone that crossed our path to ask them if they'd seen a small Yorkshire Terrier. Our hearts sank each time they shook their heads and said no.

"Travis, I'm so scared, I want her to come running out of the bushes wagging her tail and jumping into my arms."

"I'm scared too, hon, we're not going anywhere until we find her."

"What if we don't?" Claire said between tears.

"Let's not think about that and keep looking."

The path circled and we kept walking instead of turning around and heading back the way we came. It meant we'd be covering ground Slater and Sabela already had covered, or would be soon, but we wanted to be sure we left no stone unturned.

"Tilly doesn't know their voices like she knows ours," Claire said, as we kept walking.

"She's not here, Travis, she's gone," Claire cried, as I held her in my arms a few feet away from the bench where we'd agreed to meet Slater and Sabela. I looked over and saw they were there, holding hands waiting for us. They looked as sad as I felt. Sabela spotted us first and shook her head with sadness seeping from her eyes.

"Nothing Travis, and we've looked everywhere. I'm so sorry, this is awful."

"I'm not giving up yet, "Claire announced, wiping her eyes. "Maybe she'll come back home when she gets hungry."

"That's a possibility," I agreed. "What time is it anyway?"

Claire pulled her phone out of her back pocket and glanced at the screen. "Almost eleven." She rolled her eyes and hissed, "damn it, the Salvation Army will be at our place in an hour."

"Do you want to call them and cancel?" I asked, unsure if she wanted to cancel the entire move until we found out where Tilly was.

Claire shook her head, "no, this is the only time slot they have available all week. It has to be today, but I don't think I'm going to be much help."

"It's okay, you can go to your room and rest, we'll take care of everything along with Ricky and the others," Slater suggested.

"No, I want to be outside looking for her if you don't mind?" Claire replied.

I pulled her in and kissed the top of her head, "I'll look with you," I told her.

Claire rubbed her brow and wiped more tears away. "I need to sit down, I feel sick."

Sabela quickly slid closer to Slater, making room for the both of us. As we sat, Claire curled her body up into my arms and rested her head on my chest. Her tears tore at my heart and there was nothing I could say or do to make her feel better.

We all remained seated in silence with heavy hearts for some time, no one knew what to say at this point. Images of Tilly playing and running through the condo flooded my head, and her playful barks haunted my ears. "Oh, Tilly, where are you?" I whispered.

Claire's tears continued to flow, and my now damp T-shirt muffled her cries. I leaned my head back in despair and closed my eyes; it was then that I thought I heard someone call Claire's name in the distance. I opened my eyes and sat up, waiting to see if I would hear the voice again. A few seconds later the voice was closer.

"Claire!"

We all heard it that time and looked in the direction of where the sound was coming from and saw Jill running towards us, Scottie following close behind.

She called again, "Claire!" waving her arms in the air.

Claire pulled herself free from my arms and looked at Jill with a puzzled look as she waved back. "It's Jill and Scottie." Suddenly she gasped, her eyes filled with life, "Scottie has Tilly! Oh my god, he's carrying Tilly!"

I quickly stood up and focused my eyes on Scottie as Claire raced towards them. "Oh my god, he does, he has Tilly in his arms!"

Slater and Sabela stood up, and together we ran over to Jill and Scottie with smiles bigger than a Cheshire cat.

Claire reached them first and immediately took Tilly from Scottie's arms. "Tilly! Baby! I was so worried about you." Claire pulled her into her chest and laughed when Tilly smothered her face with kisses. "Where have you been, girl?"

I wrapped my arms around Claire's waist and leaned in to kiss Tilly and pet her.

"I found her," Scottie beamed with pride.

"You did?" Claire asked. "Where did you find her, Scottie?"

Slater walked over to Scottie's side and knelt beside him while Sabela took his hand. "You found Tilly?"

Scottie nodded, wearing an even bigger smile. "I sure did. She was outside on the patio sleeping under a chair."

"What?" Claire said, shocked by the news. "It never occurred to me to look out there. She never goes on the patio unless we're out there, I'm almost positive the door was closed. How did she get out?"

Scottie's smile suddenly disappeared, "I went out there to play with her, then my dad called me and I went inside."

"And you closed the door?" Slater questioned.

"Yes, because auntie Claire always tells me to, I didn't know

Tilly was still out there. Later I went back out to look for my ball and found her sleeping under the chair."

Slater rubbed the top of Scottie's head. "It's okay, buddy, you're a hero, you found her. We were all scared she was gone for good."

Scottie's smile returned, "I did? I saved the day?"

We all laughed and Tilly barked, still in Claire's arms. "You did, Scottie," Claire said with a caring smile. "You found my baby, thank you." She then turned to Jill, "I'm really sorry I went off on you for leaving the door open."

"It's okay, I deserved it. I would have never forgiven myself if Tilly never came back. When Scottie found him we raced outside, thinking you were with Logan and Sadie, they told me you were here in the park. I had left my phone in the condo and just raced over here. Besides, I wanted to see your face when Scottie showed up carrying Tilly," Jill confessed.

"I can't believe she was sleeping this whole time while we were thinking the worst. I honestly thought we would never see her again," Claire said, leaning down and kissing Tilly on the nose. "Don't you ever scare us like that again, Tilly," she said with a laugh.

"I have an idea," I announced.

"What's that?" Claire asked.

"Why don't you take Tilly over to *Open Arms* and introduce her to her new home where you can monitor her as well as helping Charlotte and Lorenzo with the food? When the Salvation Army arrives, doors may get left open and it's going to be hard to contain Tilly," I smiled. "Besides, I have a feeling you don't want to let her out of your sight for a while."

Claire squeezed Tilly, "you've got that right. I like your idea, I'll go back to the condo and grab a few things then head over to *Open Arms*."

Slater turned to Scottie and held out his hand, "give me five, buddy."

Scottie laughed and slapped his dad's hand hard. Slater then stood up and gave us all a big smile as he rubbed his hands together. "Okay everyone, are we ready to get this moving day started?"

I raised my hand, and Slater gave it a hard smack, "let's do this, bro."

CHAPTER 25

Claire

Travis was right, I wouldn't let Tilly out of my sight once we arrived at *Open Arms*. Other than Travis being in a coma for three days, I'd never been so scared in my life.

I walked the entire perimeter of the garden to make sure there was no way that she could get out, then sat down while she explored her new home. "So much for you being independent," I laughed, as she did her duty in the yard's corner.

Charlotte's presence startled me when she walked through the double French doors and then took a seat next to me, "how's she doing?" she asked.

"She's doing great, she had a nice long nap on the patio while we were searching for her everywhere in a panic," I chuckled. "It's me who's a mess. I honestly thought I'd lost her for good, I was terrified. What scared me the most was that I may never have known what happened to her; if she was found by someone and they took her home and kept her, or maybe been hit by a car or something?"

Charlotte gave me a motherly hug, something I'd been missing, and smiled, "well, you can erase all those horrible thoughts because she's home now." She looked across the yard where Tilly was sniffing the grass, "looks to me like she's enjoying her new surroundings."

"Yes, look at all the space she has, hopefully I'll train myself to not be out here all the time when she's here. I've checked every corner, and there's no way she can get out."

"Well, when you're ready to come inside, do you want to help Lorenzo and I set up the food and tables? We've enough to feed an army," she laughed. "And I've left the twins with him, he's probably ready to be relieved."

Embarrassed by my ignorance I answered quickly, feeling my cheeks flush, "yes, of course, I'm sorry, I shouldn't leave everything up to you two. Give me five minutes and I'll bring Tilly in."

"Great. Lorenzo is setting up the tables and chairs in the far garden while he's babysitting. We'll see you out there, then Tilly can check out the grounds."

"Sounds good," I replied with a nod.

Jill and Ricky were the first to arrive with a truckload of boxes from our old place, skipping through the foyer to the kitchen where I was feeding Joy and Hope.

"Where should we put the boxes?" Jill asked, "Ricky is unloading them now."

"I thought about just stacking them all in the garage, there's plenty of room. Travis and I can go through them at our leisure, that way we don't have boxes everywhere."

"Sounds good." Before walking away, she said, "hey, after we've unloaded the truck do you think I could bring Maggie over? I hate the idea of her being alone at home, it's only a ten-minute drive from here."

"Sure, that's a great idea, she can play with Tilly when she wakes up."

Jill laughed, "Tilly's sleeping?"

I pointed to her small bed under the kitchen bar where she had curled up into a tiny ball. "Yep, she wore herself out running around her new garden."

Joy let out a loud scream, startling us. "Okay, this girl wants more food; I'd help you guys, but I kinda have my hands full with these two."

Jill waved her hands, "oh, no need to help, we've got it, then we'll be back with Maggie."

Slater and Sabela arrived with little Scottie in tow as I was feeding the twins, and Sabela stayed with me in the kitchen as Slater and Scottie unloaded their truck.

"Hey girls, I missed you," Sabela said, leaning down and giving them each a kiss on their foreheads. "I hope they weren't too much trouble?"

I shook my head, "no, they've been perfect little angels, and I can't wait until our kids arrive on Tuesday. I'm so nervous, but excited at the same time; my biggest fear is that they won't like us."

Sabela returned the smile and took my hand, "they're going to love you, how could they not? You and Travis are going to be wonderful parents." She looked around the kitchen and the adjoining room, "speaking of parents, where's my mom and Lorenzo?"

"Outside in the east garden, Lorenzo's getting ready to fire up the barbecue. I've not been much help, most of my time has been spent watching the girls." I looked out the large picture window and watched Charlotte take Lorenzo's hand and kiss him on the cheek, "they sure seem happy together."

"Yeah, they're both widows and have given each other a lot of support," Sabela replied, watching her mom.

"Do you think they'll get married?"

"Oh, I don't know, I think it may be too soon for them. But I enjoy seeing my mom happy, and Lorenzo makes sure of that."

I adore how Sabela has accepted Lorenzo into their family. "And you'd be okay with it if they decide to get married one day?"

Sabela thought for a moment before answering with a nod and a caring smile, "I would. Mom and I both miss dad, and I know how much she loved him and still does, but I told her when she first started dating Lorenzo that she can't stop living. Lorenzo is not trying to replace dad, it's a new love, and it would thrill me if they got married."

"That's wonderful."

Travis and his mom Caroline arrived next with a truckload of boxes, and a few minutes behind were Logan and Sadie. Jill, who had returned with her beautiful pup Maggie, stayed in the yard with the two dogs as the rest of us teamed up to unload both trucks.

"I can help too," Sabela hollered, as she walked through the garage. "The girls are sleeping in the front room. Thank God Slater thought about bringing the playpen and some blankets," she chuckled, "I sometimes think he's a better parent than me."

Charlotte did a fantastic job setting up the long table that seated all of us, and the guys helped cook the meat, while the rest of the ladies and I served up the many side dishes everyone'd brought.

"This has been a fantastic day," Sabela said as we all sat at the table with full bellies and our drink of choice. Sabela and Slater each held a twin, and I was still having a hard time telling them apart. Sabela raised her glass, "I'd like to make a toast."

Everyone fell silent in anticipation of Sabela's toast, "I'd like to make a toast to Travis and Claire, Slater and I are so excited for the two of you. Soon you will have six children living here with you and they will be a part of your family. We couldn't have asked for a better couple to partner with. Tonight, you'll spend your first night in your new home, and tomorrow a new chapter in your lives will begin," she smiled with misty eyes. "Welcome home."

I squeezed Travis' hand and, with tears in my eyes I said, "thank you all, and thank you for believing in us."

Together, our best friends raised their glasses and yelled, "to Travis and Claire, welcome home!"

Tears ran down my cheeks as Travis pulled me in and gave me a tight squeeze, "thank you, everyone. You are correct, Sabela, I'm excited about our future, and that I'll be sharing every minute of it with the love of my life." Travis gave me a loving smile and leaned in to kiss me on the lips, "to Claire, you make my life complete, I love you so much."

I kissed him back, "I love you, too." I then turned and looked at everyone at the table, "I love all of you guys so much, you are family. Thank you for today, we couldn't have done it without you, and I sincerely mean it."

"We love you too," Jill called out, taking a sip of her wine, "but that was a lot of work, promise me you won't move again for a long time."

Everyone laughed at Jill's remark. "We promise, this will be home for a very long time."

By ten o'clock everyone had left after helping load the dishwasher and putting the leftovers in the fridge. Classic rock music played softly in the background while Travis and I crashed on the couch, and Caroline allowed her body to flop in the chair across from us.

"Man, I'm beat," Travis said, wrapping his arm around my shoulder as I rested my head on his chest.

"Me too," I replied, looking over at Caroline, "how are you doing?" I asked her.

Caroline lay back in the chair and rested her head on the back cushion,"I'm not sure, I can't feel my feet. What time are we leaving tomorrow?"

"Oh, not too early. If Tilly doesn't wake me up I plan on sleeping in."

"She has two doggie doors, remember?" Travis stated.

"After today, I'm not letting her out of my sight and she's sleeping with us tonight, I might add," I said to Travis, then added "and you don't get a say," I laughed.

Travis raised his hands in defeat, "no argument here." He then gave me a puzzled look, "where are you two going tomorrow?"

"Caroline is going to help me clean the condo, and don't forget, you need to fill the holes in the walls from our pictures and fix the closet door that came off the slider. I'm hoping to get some of our deposit back."

"Oh, that's right. Okay then, I guess we have another day at the condo."

"Let's try to make it half a day." I curled my body into his, "this is home now."

CHAPTER 26

Claire

I've never slept in such a luxurious bed in my life before, Eve had superb taste, and for the first time in a while, I slept through the entire night. no nightmares or disturbed thoughts, maybe because I'd left everything that'd been troubling me behind in the condo. And perhaps finally knowing the truth about Davin, my mind has come to accept it and is allowing me to move on and start a new life here in our new home.

I stretched my body beneath the cool 2,000 count sheets, raising my arms above my head and releasing a huge smile. My body was rested and I felt happy. I didn't know what time it was, but the sun was high in the sky, and I was alone in our enormous bed. Travis and Tilly were not in the room. I reached over and grabbed my phone from the end table and checked the time, shit! It was almost ten o'clock; I'd said I wanted to sleep in, but I've not slept this late in a long time.

After pulling myself out of bed and scrambling to find some clothes that I hadn't unpacked, I gave my face a quick wash, brushed my teeth and ran a brush through my hair. "That'll do," I said to my reflection in the mirror, leaving my room to go find the others.

I found Caroline in the kitchen emptying the dishwasher and was happy to see Tilly sound asleep in her bed close by. "Good morning, Caroline, I can't believe I slept in this late. Where's Travis?"

"He's been busy bringing in boxes from the garage and putting them in the rooms where they belong, he gave me strict orders not to wake you."

I chuckled. "Thank you, I guess I needed the rest, I slept well. What time do you want to leave for the condo?"

"Whenever you're ready, I'm almost done putting these dishes away."

"Great. Let me go track down Travis and we'll leave in about fifteen minutes; I'll take my coffee with me."

I found Travis in the garage. "Wow, you've been busy," I said, looking at the now smaller stack of boxes.

Travis turned to face me, holding out his arms, "hey wifey, you're awake," he said, taking me in his arms. "How'd you sleep?"

"Like a baby, no nightmares and I slept through the entire night," I told him.

"See, you are getting better, each day is just going to be better than the last." He kissed me passionately on the lips. His scent soothed me, and his muscular arms around my waist made me feel secure. He smiled, "are you ready to go?"

"Yes, let me grab some coffee and Tilly's leash."

Back at the condo I checked all the rooms for anything we may have left behind but found nothing except the cleaning supplies on the kitchen counter that we purposely left for today's task. The place seemed much bigger empty, and I reminisced about my last few years here. I was single when I moved in here, it was just me and Tilly and now I'm leaving as a happily married woman with the man of my dreams to start a new life with him. I smiled at the thought and left what used to be our bedroom to join the others.

Caroline already had her yellow rubber gloves on, and Travis had just entered the living room carrying his toolbox.

"Okay Caroline, I'll start in our bathroom and bedroom and let you do your room, we can do the rest together."

"Sounds great."

"We need music," Travis called from the living room.

"Hold on, let me grab my phone and I'll find something."

I laughed when I blasted my phone with classic rock and Travis moved his body in tune with the music. "Happy now?" I remarked, setting the phone on the floor and plugging it into the charger.

"Thanks, a man needs music to work by," he said, returning to fix the picture holes in the walls.

Tilly stayed close to my side as I cleaned. I periodically took her outside to do her duty, but I think it was turning into a game for her. When we lived here, she was fine with going outside every few hours, but today it seemed to be every thirty minutes.

With the bathroom finally clean I worked on the bedroom, but Tilly had other ideas and began scratching at the door which I'd closed to keep her in. "Not again, Tilly," I said as I rolled my eyes and peeled off my rubber gloves. "Okay, come on, girl, let's go."

After grabbing her leash by the door, I walked through the living room past Travis. "I'll be back, Tilly needs to go out."

Travis turned his head, "what, again?"

"Yeah, maybe this is her way of saying goodbye to this place, by leaving a lot of pee," I laughed.

"Tilly, slow down," I called as she pulled on her leash. I quickly opened the main door to the building, but as soon as I had a clear view of the steps I came to a sudden halt and froze – standing at the bottom of the steps was my mother.

"Mom, what are you doing here?"

"Claire, we need to talk."

CHAPTER 27

Claire

My mood suddenly went south. With a tight jaw I walked down the steps and attempted to walk past her, "I have nothing to say to you."

My mom grabbed my arm and squeezed it tight, taking me by surprise, "please, Claire."

I shook my arm in protest, "let go of me," I yelled, freeing my arm from her grip. "Why are you here?"

"Please, can we go inside? I don't want to talk to you out here." She paused, and I folded my arms as I waited for her to continue. "I tried to call you many times, but I couldn't get through."

"That's because I blocked you. Now, what is it you want to talk about?"

Tears pooled in her eyes, but I refused to let them get to me, "well, I'm waiting."

"Please Claire, let's go inside."

"I'm really busy, just say what you have to say and let me get on with my day."

My mom looked at the ground and clasped her hands together before looking up at me. "Very well, if you insist." She took a deep breath and then spoke, "your father is dead."

Her words echoed in my head as my knees buckled and felt as though they would give out from under me. Fearing I may fall, I switched Tilly's leash to my other hand and grabbed the metal railing next to me. "What? Dad died?" I couldn't remain on my feet any longer and lowered my body onto the concrete step, still holding the railing, "What do you mean he's dead? How did he die?"

My mom took a seat next to me and lifted her arm to embrace me, I quickly pushed her hand away and gave her a hard stare. "Don't touch me." I couldn't look at her and picked Tilly up for comfort, "when did he die and how?" I asked with a creased brow, tears trickling down my cheeks.

"He died of a heart attack on the night of your wedding. Davin's death was just too much for him, his heart couldn't take it. He was recovering from his first heart attack, but this time he didn't stand a chance."

I couldn't believe what I was hearing, "that was almost two weeks ago and you're just telling me now?" I yelled, as I quickly stood up and raced down the steps. I turned and glared at her. "Dad's been gone all this time and you didn't think about telling me?" I put Tilly on the ground and held her leash as she sniffed beneath the trees around the sidewalk.

My mom stood up but remained at the top of the stairs, "Claire, I told you I've been trying to call you, but now I find out that you've blocked me, I'm here now telling you. I'm having a small memorial for him," she said, "and also for Davin this weekend, and thought you should know."

At the sound of my brother's name, I raised my arms. "Do not speak of him after what he did to me."

My mom sniffed back her tears, "your brother didn't mean to hurt you."

I raised my voice. "I do not have a brother, mother, do you have any idea what he did to me as a child? He was a monster back then."

My mom descended two steps towards me, "Claire, what are you talking about? I'm your mother, talk to me. What did he do to you?"

I fell to my knees on the sidewalk and buried my face in my palms with Tilly at my side. "He fucking molested me, mom. He crawled into my bed naked and touched me when he was supposed to be taking care of me and watching out for me, I was just a child."

My mother gasped, racing down the steps and kneeling beside me, "why are you saying such things? He would never do that, I'm sure of it."

I wiped my salty tears away and looked at her with my eyes narrowed, "he did, mom. I don't know how many times but believe me when I tell you he did those things."

"But you never told me this before."

"Because I didn't know until last week."

My mom rubbed her brow, "Claire, you're not making any sense. How can you suddenly find out something like that? Davin is dead, I'm sure he would never tell you such things, and if you're saying you only found out last week well, he was dead so he couldn't have told you. I don't understand."

I took a deep breath. "Did you and dad take us to Sequoia National Park when we were kids? And did Davin and I share a room?" I asked in a sharp tone.

"Well yes, we did, we took you there a few times, and yes, you had the adjoining room to ours. Why?" she asked with a confused look.

"Because Travis and I went there for our honeymoon, and I had all kinds of flashbacks to my childhood. We were there." I gave her a harsh look. "Did we stay at the inn with the large chicken statue outside?"

"Yes, we did."

"And that's where we had the adjoining room?"

"Yes, Claire it is." Tears wallowed in her eyes as she reached out and touched my arm, "are you telling me that's where Davin did those terrible things?"

I nodded. "Yes mom, your son crawled into his sister's bed naked and touched her. We stayed at that inn on our last night, and I remember it like it was yesterday, I couldn't get out of there fast enough." I wiped away more tears. "I don't even know if there were other times and honestly, I don't want to know. So you see mom, Davin is not my brother, he'll always be a monster to me. Raping girls didn't start when Sabela dumped him, it started when he was a child."

"Oh Claire, I had no idea, nor did your father. Please forgive me, Claire, you're all I have. I've lost my husband and my son, I have no one else."

"Well, I lost my dad and had a monster for a brother." I looked up at the sky and wept. "I can't believe dad is gone and I want to go to his memorial, but I can't celebrate Davin's life." I shook my head vigorously, "I just can't."

My mom rested her hand on my shoulder and this time I didn't push it away. "I understand, we'll work something out, I promise. I love you, Claire, please, can you forgive me?"

"Right now I need to mourn dad, I can't do all of this at once, it's too much. Why don't you come inside and I'll put the details of the memorial on my phone. But I mean it mom, I won't go if it's a combined celebration for dad and Davin."

My mom nodded, "I'll see if I can have them separated. Maybe we can have one for your dad in the morning, then after you leave, I can have one for Davin."

I stood up and wiped the dust off my behind, "that'll work," I replied, giving Tilly's leash a little tug. "Let's go inside and you can give me the information," I said, keeping my tone flat and cold.

We walked in silence back to the condo and when I opened the door, my mom following me in, Travis turned and looked at us with a dropped jaw and wide eyes. "Abigail, what a surprise," he said, as he marched over to my phone and quickly muted it to silence the music.

My mom stood in the middle of the room and scanned the empty space, "you're moving and you weren't going to tell me? Claire, how could you?"

CHAPTER 28

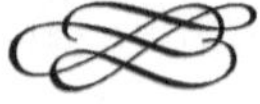

Travis

Claire ran into my arms almost knocking me over. Her tears were heavy as she sobbed into my chest, and I wrapped my arms tightly around her. "Claire, what's going on?"

"My dad died," she cried between tears.

I gasped and looked over at Abigail, "is this true?"

Claire's mom nodded, "yes, he had a heart attack on the night of your wedding. Within a few minutes of arriving home, he fell to the floor and he was gone."

Caroline must have heard Claire's sobs and joined us in the room. She came to an abrupt stop when she saw Abigail and had the same reaction as I had, "Abigail, so good to see you. Is everything okay?"

"I'm afraid Claire's dad suddenly passed away a few weeks ago," I told her.

My mom raised her hand to her jaw. "I'm so sorry. I'd offer you a seat, but as you can see we haven't any."

"It's okay, I can't stay long," Abigail replied.

Claire composed herself and raised her head from my chest, "can we hurry up and get out of here? I want to go home and lay down," she said.

"And where might home be?" Abigail asked. "I can't believe you would do this, Claire, you had no intentions of telling me, did you?"

Claire raised her hand, "please mom, not now."

Abigail ignored her. Her voice cracked when she spoke, "if I didn't come here today, you would have been gone and I would have no way of contacting you or of knowing where you went. You're all I have left, Claire."

Claire raked her hands through her hair and wiped her brow, "mom, now is not the time to talk about this, okay? Yes, I moved without telling you, but good god, you lied to me. I've been blaming you for Davin's death and I wasn't ready to have any kind of discussion with you."

"Me!" Abigail shrieked. "I had nothing to do with his death, he was my son, and I loved him, Claire. I know after what he did to those women and what he did to you, it's hard for you to understand, but as his mother I loved him unconditionally. I didn't cause his death, how could you say such a thing?"

What Abigail said shocked me. "Wait, you told your mom what Davin did to you?"

Claire nodded without looking at me, "yes, when we were outside with Tilly."

My mom looked at me with a creased brow, "did I miss something here? What did Davin do to Claire?"

I raised my hand to my mom to quiet her, "mom, I'll fill you in later." I immediately took my words back and corrected myself, "or Claire will when she's ready."

My mom softened her tone. "You know something? This

sounds like a family affair, I'm going to leave you guys alone and go back to what I was doing."

I nodded and was relieved when she left the room.

Claire pulled away from my space and stared at her mom. It upset me to see her so emotionally drained, her skin was pale, her eyes were shallow and her body was limp. "I no longer blame you for Davin's death, okay? I've been doing a lot of thinking over the past two weeks, and I've discovered a lot about myself and Davin."

"But you still blocked me on your phone, and you were planning on moving without telling me, why Claire?"

"I'm still trying to sort things out in my head, you don't know what I've gone through. I needed time before I contacted you, can't you understand that? And now I find out that dad died; I don't know how much more I can take."

Abigail clasped her hands together, "we only have each other now, Claire. Don't you think it's time we made amends and supported each other instead of fighting? I need you Claire, and I'm here for you."

Claire took a step back into my arms, "listen to your mom, sweetheart, she's right," I told Claire.

No sooner had she fallen into my arms than she quickly pushed them away, "don't, Travis. Don't rush me, I'm doing the best I can, but right now I'd like my mom to leave and for us to get the hell out of here." She shook her head and marched across the room. "Excuse me, I need a glass of water, give Travis the info for the memorial and I'll call you," Claire barked as she walked past her mother.

I didn't agree with how Claire was handling everything, but I had to let her do it her way, "okay, if that's what you want," I replied as Claire left the room and went into the kitchen.

"I'm so sorry, Abigail, I'm sure she'll come around soon, she's dealing with a lot right now."

Abigail's tone was sharp, "so am I. I lost my husband and my son on the same day, and my daughter hates me."

"She doesn't hate you."

"Can you at least try to talk to her? You're my only hope, Travis." She opened her purse and handed me a business card. "Here's the address of the memorial, will you ask her to call me in a couple of days? By then I should have the services sorted out. She doesn't want it to be a joint service for her dad and Davin, she'll only go to her dad's memorial."

"I can't say I blame her for that," I paused, "do you?"

Abigail shook her head, "no, I don't." Tears pooled in her eyes, and she sniffed them back, "I honestly did not know what Davin had done to her, she just told me when we were outside and I still can't believe it."

"It's been a shock for both of us, you should go, I think Claire has had just about all she can handle for the day."

"Promise me she'll call, or at least unblock me?"

"I'll make sure she does."

Abigail held her purse tightly to her chest as she trudged towards the front door and left me standing alone. A few minutes later, Claire came back with Tilly close behind.

"Is she gone?" she asked, taking a sip of water from the bottle she held.

"Yes, she left and said to call her in a couple of days about the memorial." I took a few steps toward her, unsure if she'd push me away again. "I'm sorry I upset you, I didn't mean to rush you, but you and your mom are both hurting."

"It's okay, I'm sorry I snapped at you."

I held out my arms, and in an instant she grabbed me and held me tightly. "I'm so sorry about your dad, Claire. Let's call it a day and head home, I think a bubble bath would do you a world of good." I rubbed her shoulders and held her in my arms, "I'll go tell my mom."

A few minutes later, after talking to my mom, I found Claire sitting on the floor with her back against the wall and Tilly laying in her lap. She looked up, "where's Caroline?"

"She had a better idea."

"What's that?" Claire asked.

"She's going to stay here and finish, then I'll come back later and pick her up. All the holes in the walls are done, and I fixed the closet door, she's just going to finish the cleaning."

"I can't ask her to do that," Claire gasped.

"You don't have a choice because she insisted." I hesitated before saying more, but I wanted to give Claire something to think about, even if it sounded harsh. "It's what family does, Claire, they support each other. Now, come on, let's get you home."

CHAPTER 29

Claire

Travis was right as usual, he always knows what's best for me. As soon as we got home, he made me a hot cup of tea and made me sit on the couch while he ran me a bubble bath.

"Now, you're not doing anything for the rest of the day but relax and pamper yourself," he told me, leading me upstairs to the master bath where the giant tub awaited.

"But we only have a week to get this house in order before the children arrive," I protested.

"We have plenty of time. Caroline will help, and Jill said she'll come after work some nights and help us unpack."

I stood in the middle of the bathroom feeling uncertain of Travis' plan, but as he undressed me, the stress I'd been feeling lightened with each button of my shirt he undid. My shoulders relaxed, and when I felt his hand rub my chest as he peeled off my top, I could feel myself melt from his touch.

I gazed into his eyes and managed a weak smile, "you're so good to me."

He returned the smile and brushed the hair away from my face. "You just relax, I'm going to take good care of you," he whispered, kissing me lightly on the neck. I remained still, my arms at my sides as he loosened my belt and unzipped my jeans. His hands felt warm against my flesh just beneath my bellybutton, and when he knelt to peel my jeans off, I rested my hands on his shoulders as I stepped out of them.

After tossing my clothes aside, Travis stood and admired me wearing only my bra and panties. He took me in his arms and caressed my back with deep strokes. "Now, you're going to soak this gorgeous body of yours and only think good thoughts, tomorrow is another day, but the rest of this day is yours." He moved his masculine hands lower down my body until they rested on my butt cheeks, giving them a good squeeze and kissing me passionately on the lips. My body became limp from his touch and I wrapped my arms around his neck.

"Will you take a bath with me?" I whispered, kissing him on the neck and tracing his jawbone with my tongue. "The only good thoughts I want to have are of you and I making love, we need to christen this amazing tub together." I gazed into his eyes and bit his lip gently, "I want to feel close to you."

I didn't need to ask Travis twice. He gave me a loving smile and glanced over at Tilly's bed and saw that she was sleeping. "Hold that thought," he said, as he walked over to the double doors of the master bedroom and closed them, then undressed as he walked back to where I stood.

Within minutes I was laying in the hot bubbly water between Travis' legs, my head resting on his chest, his arms draped over my shoulders and his hands on my chest.

"Oh, this is heaven," I moaned with my eyes closed.

Travis reached for the soap and lathered up my breasts with long, sensual strokes, "your skin is so soft," he whispered, tickling my neck with soft butterfly kisses. "And you taste so good," he chuckled as he continued to cleanse my body with the smooth soap bar, being sure not to miss an inch. My body caved to his touch, my skin tingled wherever he kissed it, and the feel of his warm tongue against my skin shot waves of lust through me.

I couldn't hold back anymore, I flipped my body until I faced him and we were chest-to-chest. Travis leaned against the back of the tub as I ran my hands through his wet hair and kissed him hard. With his arms wrapped around my waist, I whispered, "make love to me."

For the next thirty minutes I had nothing but good thoughts as Travis devoured every inch of my body and reminded me of one of the many reasons I loved him so much. Every ache, pain, headache, and negative thought that had been troubling me soon disappeared. Our lovemaking was slow and sensual, the kisses soft and long, and the many orgasms powerful and liberating.

Wrapped in his muscular arms and listening to his chest heave after he peaked, I closed my eyes, wishing I could stay in the moment forever. "This is my happy place," I whispered, "whenever I'm feeling down, we need to do this."

Travis gave my body a squeeze, "you got it, wifey, this will always be your happy place."

After a bath time to remember, Travis made sure I relaxed for the rest of the day, insisting I spend time in the garden with Tilly and a good book, which I did, and when he left to go pick up his mom, he set me up on the couch with plenty of pillows and a soft blanket, and put one of my favorite movies 'Dirty Dancing' on TV.

"I'll be back in a half hour, then I'm going to fix you dinner," he said, walking out the door.

I can't remember the last time I spent most of the day doing absolutely nothing, but judging by the way I felt the next morning, it was exactly what I needed. I woke up at the crack of dawn feeling energized and ready to face the day. My mind raced with all the things I wanted to accomplish, including calling Sabela and

Slater and going over some paperwork with them. I needed to catch up with Jill and see how the welcome party for the kids was coming along. Caroline and I planned on unpacking some boxes when she'd finished organizing her office, which reminded me that I needed to finish the filing in mine.

With the list continuing to grow in my head, I leapt out of bed and quickly came to a halt when I saw that Travis was still asleep, "shoot," I whispered as I slowed my pace and tiptoed across the room to throw on my bathrobe. I whispered to Tilly to come, before leaving the room.

Travis came downstairs an hour later and found me in my office filing papers and adding more things to my to-do list.

"Hey beautiful, you're up bright and early, you must've slept well."

I gave him an enormous grin,"I did thanks to you, and today I want to get a lot done."

"Well, it looks like you're off to a good start, I'll leave you alone."

"What are you going to do?" I asked.

"Well, first I need to get some coffee in me, then I think I'll unpack some boxes unless you need help with something?"

"No, I'm good. If you want to put the boxes in the correct rooms, I can help you, your mom and I labeled them all."

I was pleased at how the morning was going. We were all getting our tasks accomplished, upbeat music played through the surround sound, and things were coming together. I was feeling confident we'd be ready by the time the kids arrived next week.

My mood remained upbeat for most of the morning until I thought about my dad, realizing that he would never get to meet the family that Travis and I are growing together, or the children that we would welcome into our new home, or seeing our beautiful house. Travis' words from yesterday crept into my head, "it's what family do, they support each other." I knew he was referring to my mom and I, and that I should be there for her after losing dad and Davin, but I just couldn't right now. I don't know if that's wrong of me, but I needed to concentrate on myself and heal my wounds before trying to heal others, and that's what I'm doing.

The ringtone on my phone sitting on my desk startled me as I was organizing my desk. I quickly picked it up and saw that it was my doctor's office.

"Hello, Claire speaking."

"Hi Claire, this is Doctor Nelson's office, we have the results back from your blood work."

"Oh, great, what did you find out?"

"Doctor Nelson would like to talk to you in person, when can you come in?"

My heart was suddenly racing and my palms were sweating as I held the phone. "Come in?" I questioned, "I'm kind of busy, we just moved into our new home. Can't he just tell me over the phone?"

"I'm afraid not," the receptionist replied.

I started to panic about the fact that she couldn't tell me, "is it bad?" I asked, slowly sitting down at my desk.

"Doctor Nelson will share the results with you. When is a good time?"

"Well, I need to know, can I come in this afternoon?"

"Yes, of course, can you come in at two?"

"Yes, that'll be fine. I'll see you then, and Travis will be with me."

"Okay, we'll see you at two."

After I ended the call, I sat motionless in my chair for a few minutes, worried about the results of my blood test. Why couldn't they tell me over the phone? I glanced at the time on my phone. It was almost noon. God, two more hours before I would find out, this was torture.

It suddenly dawned on me that I needed to tell Travis, and immediately left my office to go find him. I called his name from the bottom of the stairs, "Travis! Are you upstairs?"

He appeared instantly and leaned over the upper landing railing, "yes, I just put more boxes in our room, do you need help with something?"

"Can you come down here? I need to talk to you," I called up to him.

It was obvious he sensed the worry in my voice by how quickly his smile disappeared, "sure," he said, quickly descending the stairs. "Everything okay?" he asked when he reached the bottom of the stairs.

"I hope so, the doctor called and said they have the results from my blood test."

"What did they say?" he asked with concern.

"They didn't tell me anything, they want to see me in person for the results, which has me worried."

Travis rested his hands on my shoulders "I'm sure it's just routine, you've been feeling fine, right?"

"Yes, I had another day of feeling queasy again, but it soon passed so I didn't bother to say anything."

Travis creased his brow, "you did? When?"

"During the party. I didn't want to ruin it for everyone, and like I said, it soon passed."

"When is your appointment?"

I took his hand and squeezed it tight. "Today at two. I didn't want to wait for days." I leaned in and Travis hugged me as I rested my head on his chest, "Travis, I'm scared."

"Me too, but whatever they tell us, we'll get through it together."

CHAPTER 30

Claire

The enthusiasm I had to get all my tasks completed soon disappeared after talking to my doctor's office, worry consumed me, and Travis, too. He ceased moving boxes around and instead made me a cup of hot tea and grabbed himself a beer to calm his nerves, which he failed to hide. Together we walked hand-in-hand to the kitchen where we found Caroline filling up Tilly's bowl of water. She turned to face us when she heard our footsteps, "hey, guess what? Tilly is using the doggie door and going in and out by herself. I can see her checking out the garden and running around on the grass, she's loving her freedom."

Travis gave her a weak smile as we both took a seat at the counter. "That's great, mom," Travis said in a flat tone, holding my hand.

Caroline stared into our eyes, "are you two okay?"

"I have to take Claire to the doctor's this afternoon, they have the results for her bloodwork, but they want to talk to her in person. You're a nurse, mom, is that normal or do they only ask you to come in person when it's bad news?"

"It depends on the practice of your doctor, some don't like to give results over the phone. They want to make sure it's the patient they're talking to, it may be their normal procedure." She patted the top of Travis' hand which was resting on the counter. "Now don't start fretting or thinking it's something terrible, I'm sure everything's fine, it's just how they run their office."

Her words lightened my mood a bit and I gave her a subtle smile. "You're probably right," I agreed, "I just hate the waiting game. I'm not a very patient person," I joked.

Caroline gave me a caring smile. "It's understandable to worry, but don't let it consume you, look at you - you look great. You have color in your cheeks, you're active and no fever, right?"

I shook my head, "no, I feel great, other than a little nervous."

Caroline slapped the countertop with her palms, "tell you what, let me grab myself an iced tea and let's take our drinks outside and watch Tilly enjoying her new yard, it'll take your minds off all this."

I smiled, "sounds like a good idea."

Travis stood first and led us outside to the patio table where we each took a seat and laughed as Tilly bounced across the grass to greet us. Travis picked up a miniature tennis ball, of which there were plenty of scattered around the garden and threw it for Tilly. We giggled again as she retrieved it and set it at Travis' feet.

"She has you trained," I laughed, as he picked up the ball and threw it again.

I glanced over at Caroline sitting across from me, "thank you, this was a good idea."

～

"See, this happens every time," I complained, pacing the waiting room at the doctor's office. "It's 2:30, our appointment was at 2:00," I hissed, sliding my phone into my back pocket for the umpteenth time since we'd arrived.

Travis was leaning forward in his seat, his arms resting on his knees, "Claire, that's the fourth time you've checked your phone. Come sit down, I'm sure they'll call us soon."

"I can't, this waiting is stressing me out."

Travis released a heavy sigh of relief when he heard the nurse call my name, "thank god," he whispered, taking my hand and greeting the nurse.

We followed her into the familiar small examination room where she took my vitals, then asked us to take a seat and said the doctor would be in soon.

After she left I rubbed my sweaty palms together and folded my arms, "I hope we don't have to wait too long, this is killing me."

Travis squeezed my hand, "I know, I'm not doing too well either. Just try to relax," he said, massaging my shoulder closest to him.

"I think they do this on purpose, make us wait like this." I scanned the room, "there's probably a hidden camera somewhere and they're watching us and laughing."

Travis slapped my thigh, "oh stop, now you're just being silly."

A light knock on the door immediately silenced us as it slowly opened and Doctor Nelson appeared.

My nerves were frayed and I shifted in my seat, wiping my sweaty palms on my pants. "Hello Doctor," I said, as I took Travis' hand.

He nodded and took a seat, "hello Claire." He turned to Travis and gave another nod, "I'm glad you came too, Travis."

"So, what's going on?" Travis asked. "Why did we need to come in person to hear the results?"

Doctor Nelson smiled, which eased me a bit, surely it can't be that bad if he's smiling I told myself.

He smiled again before he spoke. "Well, Claire, it seems you are pregnant."

I gasped, "what?"

Travis echoed my words, "what? Claire's pregnant?"

I held my hand up to my heart that was now racing as fast as my head was spinning. "But I can't get pregnant, I have PCOS."

Doctor Nelson released a slight chuckle, "yes, you do, but you still have your periods, correct?"

"Well, yes, but only two or three a year."

"Which means you are still ovulating and can get pregnant, which you are."

Tears pooled in my eyes. "I can't believe I'm pregnant, I never thought it was possible." Travis had tears in his eyes as I turned to him, "Travis, I'm pregnant, we're going to have a baby!"

Travis raked his hands through his hair, "I can't believe it."

Doctor Nelson intervened, "this is why I wanted to speak to you in person, because of your PCOS. There are some high risks related to your condition, one being that you are at a considerable risk of a miscarriage during the first trimester."

My jaw dropped. "What? Well is there anything I can do to prevent it from happening? You're scaring me, Doctor."

"We're going to do everything we can by monitoring you closely, and I'm sending you to one of the best obstetricians who is an expert in PCOS pregnancies. She's also a dietician and will work up a well-balanced diet for you and the baby. I'm also going to prescribe a medication to lower your insulin levels which is also a factor with PCOS symptoms."

"I'm in shock, I can't believe this."

Travis rubbed the back of my neck, "I'm going to take good care of you."

Doctor Nelson spoke again. "You're going to have to take good care of yourself to ensure you carry the baby to full term. Do exactly what the obstetrician tells you. You need to exercise every day; walks are good, and you need to keep any kind of stress at bay. Whatever your workload is, cut it in half immediately."

My eyes narrowed and my jawline tightened, "what? Cut my workload in half? That's going to be difficult, we just opened a Children's home and we have six kids arriving this week."

Doctor Nelson gave me a smirk, "well then, you'd better hire some help."

Travis rubbed my knee. "Don't get worked up, we'll figure something out. The most important thing is the baby."

"Yeah, you're right. I won't get myself worked up, I can't. Wow! Of all the times to get pregnant," I laughed. "I feel like I'm in a dream, can someone pinch me?" I joked.

Travis chuckled and pulled me in. "It's not a dream, Claire, we're having a baby of our own. All our dreams are coming true."

CHAPTER 31

Travis

After getting the contact and appointment information for the obstetrician from the front desk, Claire and I left the office in a daze. Still shocked by the news that we were having a baby, we walked slowly to our car in a close hug. My legs felt like jelly, and I'm sure Claire's felt the same. I was giddy with excitement that we were having a child of our own, one we'd made together, but I was nervous at the same time because of Claire's condition and the high risk involved; it would be devastating if she lost the baby.

It was when the doctor told us of the risks that I made a commitment to Claire to be there for her every step of the way during her pregnancy, we'd find a way to manage.

Claire pulled her keys out of her purse, and I quickly grabbed them from her hand. "I'll drive," I insisted.

"But you hate driving my car, you always complain that there's not enough leg room."

"Well, I'll just have to get used to it, because starting right now I'm taking care of you 100 percent."

Claire rolled her eyes and gave me a cute smile, "okay, I'm liking this."

After getting the door for her I couldn't stop smiling as I walked around to the driver's side, "I'm going to be a dad," I hollered out loud, getting in the car.

"What did you say?" Claire asked, wearing a smile as big as mine.

"I said, I'm going to be a dad."

Claire was glowing and her eyes sparkled, "and I'm going to be a mom. Oh Travis, the one thing I thought I could never give you was a child, this is a dream that I thought would never come true."

"Me too. I love you, Claire, I can't wait to get home and tell my mom that she's going to be a grandmother, she'd better be sitting down first." I suddenly had a thought and knew I had to tell Claire, even though it would dampen our moods. Before starting the car I turned to her and gave her a serious look, "Claire, you know what this means, don't you?"

"No, what?" she asked with a creased brow.

"You're going to have to tell your mom about the baby. You're carrying her grandchild, she has a right to know."

Claire leaned back in her seat and closed her eyes while rubbing her brow. "Oh, Travis, why did you have to bring her up?"

"Because it needs to be addressed, it just occurred to me when I mentioned my mom. We can't ignore the fact that your mom needs to be told about the baby, and told soon." I paused before firing up the motor, "maybe this baby of ours, who's already a miracle, will bring you two together. I think tomorrow you need to call your mom, not only to find out about the memorial, but to invite her over and tell her the news."

I felt some hope when Claire shrugged her shoulders and didn't protest, "I guess you're right, but can we not talk about it anymore? We're having a baby, and I want to lose myself in that wonderful thought while we drive home."

I leaned in and gave her a peck on the cheek, "sure, enjoy every minute."

When we arrived home we found my mom kicking back on the couch with a hot cup of tea watching 'Pretty Woman.'

"I love this movie," Claire squealed as she picked up Tilly who'd jumped out of her bed at the sound of her voice. Claire petted her as she made her way over to the couch and took a seat next to Caroline.

"So, I guess the doctor went okay?"

Claire ginned, "it went much better than expected."

"Really? So what did they tell you?"

After grabbing two bottles of water from the fridge and handing one to Claire, I took a seat on the couch with them.

"Well, don't keep me in suspense," Caroline pleaded, "what did the doctor tell you?"

My eyes met up with Claire's and we smiled, "you tell her, Travis," Claire said.

"Will one of you please just tell me," Caroline demanded, slapping the couch with her hand.

I turned to my mom and smiled, "mom, you're going to be a grandmother."

Tears pooled in Claire's eyes as we watched my mom gasp and raise her hands to her mouth, "what? Claire, you're pregnant?"

Claire nodded as she wiped away a tear. "Yes I am, we're going to have a baby."

Caroline couldn't hold back her tears as she held out her arms to me, "oh my lord, I'm speechless!"

I met my mom's embrace and held her tight, and soon Claire joined us. "I'm going to be a grandma, it's something I thought would never be possible, oh, I'm so happy for you two."

My mom pulled away from our group hug. "Now, you're going

to have to take great care of yourself Claire, and you can bet I'll make sure you do," she stated. "There are some high risks with PCOS."

"Yes, that's why the doctor wanted us to come in so he could go over them with us. One is that there is a considerable risk of a miscarriage during the first trimester."

I took my mom's hand, "don't you worry mom, between you and I we will make sure Claire does everything she's supposed to."

My mom suddenly threw her head back into the pillows of the couch, "oh my, what timing this baby has, a week before we have six kids arriving. It's crucial you take it easy Claire, and not work too hard. Boy Travis, we certainly have our work cut out for us."

"We'll manage, mom. If we have to, we'll hire some extra help, but let's see how it goes first."

CHAPTER 32

Claire

The next morning I woke up to Travis looking down at me and smiling, his head resting on his hand. "How long have you been looking at me?" I said in a sleepy voice.

"Long enough to think about what an amazing mom you're going to be to our child." He rested his free hand on my belly, "how are you feeling?"

I chuckled, "I feel fine. Are you going to ask me that every ten minutes?" I joked, "like you did last night?"

"Well, this is nothing to mess around with. If you're not feeling well, let me know so I can take care of you."

"I will, I promise."

"I'm telling you this because you were sick at the party and didn't tell me."

"Well, I didn't know I was pregnant then." I caressed his hand, "Travis, I'm concerned about the risks involved just as much as you are, and I am going to do everything in my power to prevent anything from happening. I'll do everything the doctor tells me and then some, we're not going to lose this baby. We also have your mom living with us who's a registered nurse, and if you take after your mom, then I am in excellent hands."

"That's my girl." He paused for a moment and then spoke again, "now for the bad news."

I sat up, concerned by his tone, "what bad news?"

"Today you have to call your mom, the sooner you talk to her, the better. Remember, you need to keep stress at bay, and the tension between you and your mom could be cut with a knife. I know it's caused you a lot of stress and will continue to do so if you don't take care of it. It's not good for the baby, or you for that matter, please tell me you'll call her today?"

I knew Travis was right, and when he mentioned I could put the baby at risk if I didn't do something, I realized I had no choice, "I agree with you."

Travis raised his eyebrows, "you do? Well that was easy."

"I'm going to unblock her from my phone and call her. I don't want to tell her about the baby over the phone, that just doesn't seem right. In fact, I'd rather not be alone with her when I tell her."

"You don't?" Travis asked, looking confused.

I folded my arms and leaned back against the headboard of the bed, "I don't know why, but I don't want it to be so intimate when I tell her, I want the support of you and our friends around me. What I should say is that I need you all to be there. I'm not sure if I'm making any sense, but I'm just not ready to be alone with my mom."

Travis smiled, "it makes sense, just take baby steps and rebuild your relationship with your mom slowly at a pace that works for you. Taking the first step will be the hardest, but I'm here for you."

I returned the smile, "thank you for understanding." I placed my hands in my lap and took a deep breath. "What do you think about us going to my dad's memorial and then inviting her over here for dinner this weekend? I want to invite the rest of the gang as well, that way we can tell everyone at once."

"I love that idea, you must have been giving this some thought before I brought it up."

I felt my cheeks blush, "I admit, it's crossed my mind, and yes, I thought about it all last night."

It took me a few hours to build up enough courage to finally take the first steps in rebuilding my severed relationship with my mom. After Travis and Claire informed me that I could no longer drink coffee, Travis handed me a protein shake and a bowl of fresh fruit to start my day, which I ate while checking the messages on my phone and taking notes. Then, with Travis sitting next to me on the couch, I unblocked my mom and dialed her number.

The phone rang a few times before she answered, and I spoke in a flat tone, "hello mom, it's Claire, you're no longer blocked on my phone."

My mom's voice shook when she replied, "thank you Claire, I appreciate that. I could change the memorial and have it just for your dad in the morning, then we will have one for Davin thirty minutes later which gives you enough time to leave."

I reached out and held Travis' hand, "thank you, when is it?"

"The day after tomorrow at 9:00 AM," my mom replied.

"Okay thanks, we'll see you then." I had no other words and attempted to end the call. "Goodbye." But before I could, she spoke again.

"Claire, I'm really sorry about everything and I hope that one day you'll forgive me."

My hands shook as I raced to get out my next words, "I have to go mom," quickly ending the call before dropping the phone on the coffee table. "God, that was hard," I said as I tried to calm my racing heart.

"Calm down, Claire, you took the first step. Now take some deep breaths and relax, you did great," Travis told me in a soothing voice.

"The service for my dad is in two days which gives me enough time to prepare and call the others before they make any plans for the weekend."

Travis pulled me in and held me close. "My mom and I will call everyone and make it an early dinner. No more late nights for you, you need plenty of sleep every night, and you're not cooking either."

"So, what are we going to have?"

"I'll have my mom find a place that delivers healthy food, something you can eat. Leave it to us, we'll take care of everything," he smiled, "I'm going to make this as stress-free as possible, wifey."

CHAPTER 33

Claire

When we pulled up to the building where my dad's services were being held, I spotted my mom right away, standing outside dressed in a black dress greeting the guests. I recognized a few people as some of his co-workers before he retired.

After shutting off the motor Travis reached over and rested his hand on my knees, "are you ready?" he asked.

I continued to stare out of the window and ran my hands over my grey skirt, "as ready as I'll ever be, let's do this."

Travis took my hand as we walked slowly towards my mom. She spotted us before we reached her and raised her hand slightly, giving us a nervous smile. "She looks as nervous as I feel," I whispered.

"That's because she probably is," Travis whispered back.

"Thank you for coming, Claire," my mom said as we both stood face-to-face with our arms limp. Neither one of us made a move to give the other a hug.

"He was my dad, mom. There's no need to thank me, I'm here for him."

She nodded, "Of course," and gestured with her hands for us to go inside. "I'll be in soon, I want to stay here for a few more minutes and greet everyone."

"Sure, we'll see you inside," Travis replied as he led me through the door.

It was a small gathering of people, some I didn't know, but a few I recognized as long-time friends. Travis held my hand as we made our way up to the front where there was a photo collage of my dad's life. A few were family photos when we were a happy, normal family. "I'll miss you, dad," I whispered, as I smiled at a picture of me around the age of four sitting on dad's knee, "you were a wonderful dad."

Travis squeezed my hand, "are you doing okay?"

"Yeah, just talking to my dad, he didn't deserve this. It's because of Davin that he died, and I blame him for dad's death."

"You have a right to feel that way, do you want to go sit down?"

"Yeah," I replied, wiping away a tear.

While we sat and waited for the services to begin, a few people who recognized me approached us and gave me their condolences. I couldn't remember their names or how I knew them, but shook their hands as I thanked them.

My mom joined us a little while later, and during most of the service we remained silent until she asked me if I wanted to say a few words. I quickly shook my head, "I can't, I'm sorry, I'm too nervous."

My mother patted my knee and I froze from her touch, "that's okay, I felt I should ask you. Excuse me, it's time for my speech."

Guilt swept over me as I watched my mom take the stage alone. Her hands shook as she attempted to straighten out her notes, and before she even spoke, tears flooded her eyes and ran down her cheeks. "I'm sorry, please just give me a minute," she sobbed, as she attempted to wipe her face with a tissue and compose herself.

I had never seen my mom look so alone and scared, and it tore at my heart, what was I doing? I let go of Travis' hand, "I'll be right back."

Travis gave me a confused look, "where are you going?"

"Where I should be."

When I stood, I felt all of the heads in the room turn and look my way. I didn't make eye contact with anyone as I made my way up to the front of the room and took my mom into my arms as she wept, "it's okay, mom, I'll help you get through this, dad would be so proud of you."

Still crying heavily, my mom whispered, "thank you," as I held her tight in my arms and looked over at Travis who had tears in his eyes and smiled with pride.

After a few moments my mom was able to pull herself together, and as she read from her notes, I held her close, and laughed and cried along with her as she shared memories of the man she had loved for most of her adult years. When she had finished, I felt the sudden need to share a few words and some fond memories of the wonderful dad I had lost. I made it short and ended by saying, "I'm going to miss you so much, dad. You taught me so much, and I am who I am today because of you." I turned and looked at my mom, "and I promise you dad, I will take care of mom, she's going to be okay."

After hearing my words, my mom looked into my eyes and whispered, "I love you."

I smiled, and through my tears I held her tight and whispered, "I love you too, I'm so sorry," and led her back to our seats where Travis was wiping away more tears.

He smiled and took my hand before kissing me on the lips, "I'm so proud of you."

"I listened to my heart and did exactly what it told me to do.

No more fighting, we're family, and family support each other, right?"

Travis let out a small laugh, "right."

He turned to my mom and praised her for her speech and gave her an affectionate rub on the shoulder.

"I couldn't have done it without Claire, if she hadn't come up I would have totally lost it."

We remained seated while my mom mingled with some of the guests, and those that were staying for Davin's services took their seats again.

I nudged Travis' elbow, "it's time for us to go."

"Okay," Travis said, standing. "Let's go say goodbye to your mom and tell her about Saturday."

I followed Travis over to my mom who was talking to a couple her age and patted her shoulder, "sorry mom, I don't mean to interrupt, but we have to get going."

"Thank you for coming and for saving me up there."

"It's okay mom, no need to thank me. Listen, I want to invite you to dinner at our new house this Saturday, will you come?"

Her eyes lit up, "I would love to."

"Great, I'll call you tomorrow and give you the address, we'll see you then."

"We're going to be okay, aren't we Claire?"

I took my mom's hand and nodded, "I think so."

CHAPTER 34

Travis

What I witnessed today at the memorial service was unexpected. Claire did what she'd told me and listened to her heart instead of allowing her anger to dominate her.

We've both made drastic changes in our lives in just a few days since we found out Claire was pregnant. We've taken long walks around the neighborhood with Tilly every night and changed our diets by eating more healthy foods. My mom insists on cooking the meals and cleaning the house, while Claire takes care of her office work and lighter tasks.

The only thing that was causing stress in our lives was the relationship she had with her mom, or lack of it, and the resentments she held against her, blaming her for many things. Claire knew it too, and still held a grudge the night before the services, which had me concerned when I told her she couldn't get worked up when she was with her mom.

"I'll do my best, okay?" she snapped, "but you're asking for a damn miracle."

Seeing Claire getting worked up, I immediately dropped the conversation and turned on the TV.

Claire soon calmed down, and for the rest of the night we relaxed on the couch with Tilly snoozing between us.

Since the services, we've been able to talk about her mom without Claire getting upset, and I can see that Claire's smiles are genuine when she talks about the upcoming dinner.

"I called my mom this morning and gave her our address and I told her to come a half-hour after everyone else arrives," Claire told me when I peeked my head through the door of her office.

I creased my brow, "why did you do that?"

"Because I want to give everyone a heads up that she'll be here. I don't want my mom to walk into a room of shocked and frozen faces, they all know my relationship has been strained with her."

"That's probably a good idea, it's good to see you happy and relaxed."

She leaned back in her chair and smiled, "I am happy. I feel great and it feels so good not to walk around so uptight and with a sour taste in my mouth."

"That was a great thing you did yesterday, you should be proud of yourself, it took a lot of guts to walk up there."

"It really didn't, I think my dad was there helping me."

I smiled, "he was." I checked my pocket for the truck keys. Okay, I'm off to the store, can I leave it to you to call everyone and invite them for dinner?"

"I'm on it."

I left Claire feeling good about our future and fired up the truck, grinning like a Cheshire cat as I backed out of the driveway. I've always wanted a big family, and in just under a week we'd would be welcoming six beautiful children with open arms and lots of guidance and love. Then I began thinking about the baby and yelled at the top of my lungs, "I'm going to be a dad!" All my dreams were coming true, even my mom is now in my life, and she'll be here to help raise our child, her grandchild. I shook my head at all the goodness that was happening in not only my life, but Claire's and my mom's, too. So many of our dreams were being fulfilled. When people tell me that life is good, I now know what they mean.

CHAPTER 35

Claire

Travis wasn't joking when he told me he was going to take good care of me, he wouldn't let me do anything. It's actually kind of cute, he's been leaving most of the paperwork and business phone calls up to me, but everything else he was doing with Caroline's help.

We saw the obstetrician yesterday, and I left feeling more positive about the pregnancy after leaving her office. She certainly had the experience and knowledge for treating women with my condition and answered all our questions. We left with a folder full of suggested foods, exercises to do and how to manage my health. She said she would call me weekly to schedule an in-office appointment every week during the first trimester so that she could closely monitor me.

Caroline and Travis had taken care of everything for the dinner party tonight. Caroline did an amazing job setting the large dining room table, complete with fancy cloth napkins, fine silverware and seamless wine glasses, and even a bouquet of sunflowers surrounded by white floating candles in a crystal bowl.

"Wow Caroline, you went all out, the table looks beautiful."

"Well, it's not every day you get to invite your best friends over for dinner and announce you're pregnant, it's a special occasion and we should treat it that way."

"You're right, thank you." I glanced over at the kitchen counter and saw the serving bowls, "so what's for dinner?"

We're having shrimp cocktail, Hawaiian chicken and rice, a fresh fruit salad and a steamed vegetable platter, it should be here anytime."

"Sounds delicious," I said, glancing at the gigantic clock on the wall and seeing I had thirty minutes to freshen up before people began arriving. "I'm going to run upstairs and freshen up, Travis is already changing. Would you mind feeding Tilly?"

"No problem, go right ahead. I'm waiting for the food to be delivered."

Travis was already dressed in loose beige slacks and a white shirt, unbuttoned down to his chest with the sleeves rolled up midway. I stood in the doorway of the master bath and admired his behind as he stood in front of the mirror splashing on cologne.

"Damn your ass looks good in those pants, and you smell delicious too," I said, breathing in his scent.

He winked at me while looking at the mirror, "why thanks, wifey."

I walked up to him and wrapped my arms around his waist from behind, "did you see the table your mom set for dinner? It looks fantastic."

"I did, and she told me that tonight was a special night, so I thought I would dress for the occasion."

I looked down at my attire, jeans and a tank top were not cutting it, "I guess I should do the same."

I finally decided on a pair of light blue dress pants and a white lace shirt, finishing my outfit off with a silver horseshoe necklace. After applying some light makeup and brushing my hair, Travis gave me a wolf whistle from the bedroom, "you are one hot mama," he called.

I turned and blew him a kiss, "I'll be right there."

By the time we returned downstairs, the food had been delivered and Caroline was busy dishing it up into the serving dishes she'd laid out.

"Let me help you, mom," Travis said as he picked up a box of food.

"Me too," I added, I felt useless.

Between the three of us we managed to get the food on the table in no time and cover the hot food with matching lids to keep it warm. Travis poured himself and his mom a glass of wine and gave me a glass of Perrier. No sooner had we sat down on the couch than the doorbell rang.

"I'll get it," I said, setting my drink down and heading to the front door, finding Slater and Sabela on the other side holding the twins with Scottie standing between them.

I held out my arms and greeted them both with a friendly hug, kissing each of the baby girls on the top of their heads, "I still can't tell them apart," I laughed.

"This is Joy," Sabela said, "and Slater has Hope."

"I'm glad you made it, come on in."

Sabela entered first and glanced around the colorful front room that was super kid friendly. "Wow, the house looks fabulous, you've been busy."

Slater stood next to her and admired the lockers and benches with each child's name on it. "This is fantastic, did Travis make this?"

"He sure did."

"Damn, I miss his craftsmanship, I'm glad to see he's still got it."

I led them into the front room, "you're the first to arrive, the others should be here shortly." I looked over at Travis, "honey, would you get them a drink?"

Sabela's mom and Lorenzo arrived next, then Logan and Sadie. As expected, Ricky and Jill were the last to arrive and were even fifteen minutes late, but I was pleased to see they'd brought Maggie with them, and so was Tilly who ran to the front door like a rocket to greet her.

"Aww look, they remember each other," Jill said.

"Let's put them out back where they'll have the whole yard to run around in."

"Good idea," Jill said, guiding both dogs over to the double French doors.

Once everyone was gathered in the living room mingling and sipping their drinks, I asked them for their attention. The room quickly fell silent, and all eyes focused on me, the only person standing.

"Thank you all for coming, we're waiting for one more guest to arrive, and she should be here any minute. I wanted to give you a heads up on who it is so that there are no surprises. I felt she should be here too for this special night."

"Well, who is it?" Jill called across the room, "the Queen of England!?"

Everyone laughed, and I allowed the room to quieten down before revealing who it was.

"No, it's my mom."

"Oh wow," Jill said, taking a large gulp of her wine.

"So you and your mom are okay now?" Sabela asked.

"We're working on it. A lot has happened this week, and I haven't seen any of you to tell you, but my dad died of a heart attack the night of our wedding."

The room immediately echoed with sorries and gasps, and I immediately looked over at Slater. "I blame no one, dad already had a weak heart, and everything that happened that night was just too much for him. I went to his memorial this week ,and let's just say that my mom and I are working on our relationship, and I felt it only right that she should be here tonight."

"So sorry about your dad, Claire," Jill said. "So, what's the special occasion? You've got the fancy table, and both you and Travis are all dressed up."

"You'll find out soon enough. In the meantime, keep mingling and drinking," I said with a laugh.

"Oh, I hate waiting, you're such a tease," Jill said, high-fiving Scottie who'd raised his hand to her, then getting a high-five from the others.

While I was playing with the twins surrounded by soft toys Scottie had brought up from the playroom, the doorbell rang. "That's my mom," I told Sabela as I handed her the toy I was holding, "I'll be right back."

Before opening the door, I took a deep breath and ran my fingers through my hair. "Everything's going to be okay," I whispered under my breath, pulling the door open and giving my mom a caring smile. I held out my arms and gave her a hug, "hey mom, I'm glad you made it."

"I wasn't sure if I had the right address, this isn't a house Claire, it's a mansion."

She entered the foyer and gazed at the large, bright chandelier, "my god, this place is gorgeous, you've done well, Claire."

"It's not our house, mom, you know that. It's Slater and Sabela's, we're business partners."

"Yes, I know, but this place is amazing."

"Yes, it is. Now come on, everyone's here, why don't we go say hello? They're all eager to see you."

My mom stalled. "Really? I thought they would all hate me after, well you know, Davin and all."

I took her arm, "mom, no one hates you, okay? I told them about dad and, just like me, they're here for you, too. We're all healing from that dreadful night, but these are my friends, and they want to be yours, too."

"Thank you, Claire," my mom said as I led her to the others.

"Everyone, you all remember my mom?"

Sabela's mom Charlotte was the first to speak, "Abigail, it's so good to see you, I'm so sorry to hear about your husband, Jeffery. If there's anything I can do, please let me know."

My mother spoke in a quiet voice, "thank you, I appreciate that."

One by one my friends made me proud by making my mom feel welcome, and I felt at ease as I noticed my mom relaxing. She left my side to go admire Joy and Hope playing contently at Sabela's feet. There were even a few words shared with Slater; I'm not sure what they said, but when I saw them smile at each other my heart rate slowed.

"Okay everyone, let's gather around the table. The food's getting cold, and after dinner Travis and I would like to make a toast."

"Are you going to finally tell us what the special occasion is?" Jill asked, walking across the room.

"Yes Jill, I will."

I was pleased to see that Caroline had thought ahead and brought up two highchairs from downstairs for Joy and Hope.

"One good thing about running a Children's home is that you won't have to bring anything for the twins when you visit, we have everything here," I told Sabela, who sat across from me with Travis and my mom on either side.

"That makes it much easier, I can't believe the stuff we have to lug around."

During dinner I took a moment to glance around at everyone at the table laughing and chatting with each other. Smiles and laughter were plentiful, and the atmosphere in the room was that of one big happy family which, in my mind, we were. They were the first people I turned to for help, advice, or just an enjoyable time. I turned to Travis, took his hand, and smiled, "do you think it's time?" I whispered in his ear.

He squeezed my hand, "yes, it's time."

"Okay everyone, this is probably the last adult meal we'll have in a long time," I announced across the table in a loud voice. Everyone suddenly stopped talking and listened to what I had to say. "As you know, in a few days we will welcome six children into our home and will raise them as our own until someone offers them a forever home. If that doesn't happen, they will remain with us until adulthood if need be, we will not allow any child that comes to us to be shuffled around in the system.

Everyone raised their glasses and cheered at our commitment. I stared at Jill when I spoke next, "how are the welcome party plans coming along? Do you need any help?"

Jill sat up straight, pride beaming from her eyes, "nope, I have it all under control and they'll be here at 11:00 AM. I've invited everyone, and I'll be here at 9:00 AM to set up. Anyone that wants to be here, I'll have plenty for you to do."

I wasn't surprised when Jill was suddenly swarmed with offers of help from everyone, agreeing to be here at 9:00 AM.

"You guys are amazing," I hollered across the table, "thank you!" I took a deep breath and looked at Travis before I spoke, "there is one more thing I want to tell you, which is why we are also all here tonight."

"Ooh, this is it," Jill squealed.

"Jill, be quiet, let Claire speak," Sabela pleaded.

Jill lowered her head, "sorry."

"Okay, now that I have your attention, I wanted to let you know that there will be one more child living with us, he or she will be arriving a little later than the others."

Slater creased his brow, "another child? I haven't heard anything about that." He looked at Sabela, "did you know?"

Sabela shook her head, "no, this is the first I'm hearing of it, when did you agree to a seventh child?"

"Well, we didn't exactly agree. It kind of landed in my lap, and I literally mean it when I say landed in my lap."

"What?" Sabela said, "I don't understand."

A big smile blanketed my face as I continued, "what I'm trying to say is that I'm pregnant, we're having a baby." I turned to my mom and took her hand, "mom, you're going to be a grandmother."

CHAPTER 36

Claire

The table immediately erupted into screams of joy and gasps of shock.

Jill's high-pitched squeal was heard above everyone else's, "oh my god, you're frigging pregnant!" Her eyes were wide as she clapped her hands and did a dance in her seat. "You mean I'm going to be an aunty again?"

I tossed my head back with joy, "Yes Jill, you will be our baby's aunt."

Sabela leaned back in her chair and held her hand up to her chest, "wow Claire, this is amazing news, especially when you thought you couldn't get pregnant, I'm so happy for you both."

"It's truly amazing, we still can't believe it because as you know I have PCOS, and the chances of me getting pregnant were very slim, but here we are."

I turned to my mom who still hadn't said a word and seemed to be in a daze. I took her hand, 'mom, did you hear me? You're going to be a grandma."

She looked at me with glazed eyes, "I can't believe it, Claire, you're going to have a baby."

"Yes, I am mom. This baby is a miracle, I guess I just needed to be with the right man to make it happen."

"Oh Claire, I wish your father was here, he would have been an amazing grandfather."

"Me too, mom, but I'm sure our child will have some of dad's traits."

Travis leaned in and rested his head on my shoulder as he looked over at mom, "How are you doing, Abigail? Can you believe it?"

"I'm in shock; me, a grandmother, I never thought it would happen. Thank you both for letting me be a part of this special moment and a part of this baby's life."

I gave my mom's hand another squeeze, "it's how it should be, I don't want our child to miss out on anything, and that includes you."

Logan and Sadie cheered out loud along with Jill and Ricky, hugging Travis' mom Caroline who sat close to them and congratulated her because she, too was going to be a grandmother.

Slater smiled from across the table and raised his glass, "I want to make a toast to two amazing people that beat the odds and will be incredible parents, to Claire and Travis, congratulations. And might I add Hope and Joy can't wait to meet their new playmates."

The table echoed with cheers, and I hugged my mom, who was now crying heavily. "Thank you, guys, I love you all. Travis and I are still trying to take all this in, we only found out earlier this week and we're still in shock. Because of my condition, we never thought in our wildest dreams we could have a child of our own, so you can only imagine how elated we are."

"I'm in shock too," Sabela agreed. "How on earth are you going to manage carrying the baby and running *Open Arms*?" She released a slight chuckle, "I know you're a strong woman Claire, and a hard worker, but wow! You two are going to have your hands full, do you need help?"

"Trust me, we have been asking the same question all week, and because of my PCOS there are very high risks involved."

The table fell quiet, "like what?" Sabela asked.

I took a deep breath, "well, what is most concerning is that I'm at a high risk of having a miscarriage during the first trimester."

"Oh, no!" Jill cried as more gasps followed from the others.

"Is there a way to prevent that from happening?" Slater asked.

Travis spoke next, wrapping his arm around my shoulders, "Claire will be closely monitored, and the doctor has put her on medication to reduce her insulin levels. She is now on a very strict diet and must not strain herself, physically or mentally. Our number one priority is making sure Claire can carry our child to term, and between me and my mom, we'll do whatever it takes. If it means hiring extra help, then we'll do that, and from our work-load and Claire's condition, that's what we need to do.

Jill suddenly protested, "oh no you don't."

I gave Jill a hard stare, "excuse me Jill? Why are you objecting to us hiring help? We can't do it all."

"If you're going to hire anyone it's going to be me."

Ricky suddenly turned and looked at Jill, "what? You already have a job."

"Yeah, and I hate it. Being around kids would be much more fun than grumpy patients that already hate the dentist and take it out on me." Jill clasped her hands together and began begging, "please guys, let me help you."

I was stunned by Jill's offer. "Wow Jill, I don't know what to say. Are you sure? You'd be around kids all day."

"Yes, of course. Why wouldn't I be? Sabela and Slater are around theirs all day and they're doing great."

"But those are their kids. There's a significant difference, it's like comparing apples to oranges."

"Then this would be good practice for me when Ricky and I have kids of our own," quickly gave Ricky a stare, "which won't be for a while. Please guys, I'd love to do it," she pleaded, clasping her hands together again.

My mom suddenly spoke, "I'd like to help, too."

Again, I was stunned, I wasn't expecting these offers and was touched. "You would?"

"Of course, you're my daughter and you're carrying my grandchild, and now that your father is gone, I need a purpose in life and to feel needed, please let me help you both."

I leaned back in my seat and shook my head, "wow, I don't know what to say, what do you think, Travis?"

"Please," Jill begged from across the table.

"It's up to you, babe. One thing I want to point out though is that we know Jill and your mom far better than any stranger we might hire, and they're family," he grinned at Jill, "even Jill."

Jill returned the grin, "I agree with Travis, we're family."

"Well, we'll definitely need help with the younger kids that aren't in school, they'll have to be supervised and entertained all day."

"I can do that, we can take them on field trips, do crafts and play games," Jill announced in a loud voice.

I continued with our needs. "And we can't expect Caroline to do all the cooking, she's the nurse, and we can't take her away from that."

"I love to cook, Claire. When you were small, I used to cook all the time. I miss those days and would enjoy cooking big meals again. We could even plan menus together for the week."

"Really mom? It wouldn't be too much for you?"

"Caroline and I can help her, too. I bet Travis is good in the kitchen as well," Jill suggested. "Come on Claire, it will solve all your problems, and as Travis mentioned, it's better to hire family than strangers."

I hesitated for a moment as I ran everything through my mind.

Could this really work? I asked myself. The tension in the room was high, everyone was quiet as they waited for my decision.

"Well Claire, what do you think?" Travis said in a way that I understood. His pleasant tone told me he liked the idea as much as I did.

"Well, I guess the only thing left to say is, Jill, mom, welcome aboard *Open Arms*."

Jill's jaw dropped, "really? You mean it? I can work for you?"

"Yes Jill, when can you start?"

"Shit, I'm handing in my notice Monday. When do the kids arrive?"

"Tuesday," Travis said.

Jill waved her hands. "Oh, then I just quit," she laughed. "I'll call them Monday and let them know, then I can be here Monday morning so we can go over everything." She rubbed her hands together and gave Ricky a hug, "I'm so excited."

My mom hugged me with tears in her eyes, "thank you, Claire. This will be good for us, I know it will."

"Yes it will, mom. *Open Arms* doesn't just welcome children, but also family."

CHAPTER 37

Claire

Jill did what she said she was going to do and quit her job Monday morning. When she arrived at our house shortly after my mom at noon, she came bursting through the door beaming. "Oh, I can't tell you how good it feels to be rid of that place! I dreaded being there every day, it was such a depressing job. People crying in pain with a toothache or coming in to get dentures, ugh, good riddance."

I laughed at Jill's remarks, "well, here you'll be surrounded by young, cheerful kids and you'll feel good about yourself because you'll be improving their lives."

Jill nodded in agreement, "you've got that right."

After giving her and my mom a walk through and a rundown of *Open Arms* I was feeling good about having them be a part of the crew. I could tell Travis was too, by the way he smiled and agreed to some of their ideas and the excitement in his voice when we sat down and shared the kids' files.

"They're all so beautiful," my mom said. "What you and Travis are doing for them is wonderful, I can't wait to meet them."

"Well, tomorrow morning the three youngest will arrive, Colin, Matthew and Kate, then on Wednesday we welcome Jasmine, Nicole and Janet."

"Oh, this is so exciting!" Jill cried. "And I have everything arranged for the party on Saturday, it's going to be so much fun."

"It is, I just hope I can sleep tonight. As excited as I am, I'm also nervous as hell, I have this terrible feeling I can't shake that the kids won't like us."

Travis chuckled, "oh, not that again, Claire. The kids are going to love you, and this house, my mom, Jill and Abigail, too, quit worrying." He looked over at his mom writing some notes in one of her files on the couch where we all sat. "Can you tell her mom? She won't listen to me."

"He's right, Claire, you've made a beautiful home here for them. Look where they're coming from, you have nothing to worry about. Just embrace them and love them, that's all they need."

As feared, I barely slept last night and was up and out of bed by 6:00 AM, only to find Travis' side of the bed empty. After putting on my bathrobe I headed downstairs where I found Travis and his mom sitting at the counter drinking coffee. I chuckled, "I see you couldn't sleep either."

"Nope, but with the big day ahead I'm not even noticing my lack of sleep," Travis said, giving me a hug and a peck on the cheek.

"Me neither," Caroline said with a nod.

I leaned in and smelled the aroma of Travis' coffee, "god that smells good."

"Well, that's all you get is the aroma, your smoothie's in the fridge."

I rolled my eyes, "thanks," and walked to the fridge to grab my healthy morning drink.

Jill and my mom arrived five minutes apart around 8:00, and my mom immediately went to work with Jill and Caroline to prepare healthy snacks for the children when they arrived.

"Why am I so nervous?" I said, checking the time on the wall again and continuing to pace the room. It was almost 9:00, the children would be here anytime now.

Travis left his seat at the kitchen bar and approached me, "just relax," he said, rubbing my shoulders. "Everything'll be fine."

I suddenly jumped when the doorbell rang, and my jaw dropped. I gasped as I stared into Travis' eyes, "they're here."

Everyone froze. "This is it," I said, trying to calm my racing heart, "our children are here."

Jill, my mom and Caroline joined Travis and I in the front room. "Let's go meet them," Travis said with a loving smile, taking my hand and leading me to the front door with the others following closely behind.

As soon as Travis opened the door, all of my anxieties quickly disappeared as I stared into the frightened eyes of the three children. Why had I been so afraid? I thought to myself, they're just helpless young children that are probably more afraid than I am.

A middle-aged woman stood next to them and gave us a charming smile. "Hello, I'm Doris, the social worker, I'm sorry we're a little late, there was a lot of traffic. She tapped the closest boy's head next to her, "this is Collin."

I smiled, "hello, Collin."

He looked up and gave me a weak smile, "hi."

"And this is Matthew," Doris continued, tapping his head.

Travis knelt and smiled at the boy, "hello, Matthew."

Matthew avoided eye contact, "hello."

"And finally, this is Kate."

"Hi Kate. Why don't you all come in and meet everyone, then we can sit down and have some snacks and get to know each other?" I said in a gentle voice.

Jill and the others moved away from the door so the children could come in, greeting them with friendly smiles and soothing voices as Travis and I attended to business with Doris.

"Let's go in the front room," Caroline suggested. "We have all kinds of snacks for you, then we'll show you your new home."

After going through the necessary paperwork, Travis unloaded the children's luggage from Doris' car. It saddened me when I saw just three small bags lined up on the sidewalk, this was everything they owned.

"Thank you Doris, for everything. We'll see you tomorrow, we can't wait to meet the rest of the children," Travis said as she got into her car and drove off.

Travis refused to let me carry any of the luggage, and once he'd placed them at the bottom of the stairs we headed into the front room to join the others. My heart immediately lifted when I saw Jill playing bumper trucks with Matthew and Collin. They were both smiling and laughed every time they crashed their cars into Jill's. My laugh matched theirs as Matthew smashed his truck again and Jill cried "ouch! You hurt my truck," causing Matthew to laugh louder.

"Look how good Jill is with them, I had no idea," I whispered to Travis.

I glanced over at my mom sitting on the couch with Kate helping her color a picture. She too was smiling when she held up her favorite color crayon.

I leaned into Travis' space and closed my eyes as he embraced me, "what a beautiful sight this is."

"It sure is, come on, let's go join our family."

CHAPTER 38

Travis

That saying that a woman glows when she's pregnant is so true, I kid you not. Claire has been glowing since the day we found out she was carrying our child, and as I sit here with her wrapped in my arms along with our six children who've joined our family, I see her blossoming.

Yesterday we spent the entire day with Jill, Abigail and my mom making sure the first three children felt welcome and comfortable in their new home. Tilly also played a big part and soon became their best friend. We showed them their rooms and told them that everything in them was theirs; their eyes lit up when we said they could decorate their rooms with all the things they liked.

We were shocked by how good Jill was with kids; we had no idea, I'm not even sure if she knew, but she warmed up to the kids like she'd been around them all her life and made them feel at ease in no time. She spent the afternoon painting and drawing with them and writing ideas down for their rooms. Before she left it was touching to see each child reach out to her and ask for a hug.

That evening after the house had quieted down and all the kids' bellies were full, we all nestled on the couch, including my mom, and spent our first night together watching Disney movies. The two youngest, Collin and Matthew, curled up with Claire and I, while Kate rested her head in my mom's lap.

"Look at us Claire," I whispered, "this was a dream of ours not so long ago and here we are living it."

Claire gave me a loving smile, "I think I'm the happiest woman in the world, I love you so much."

"I love you too," I said, kissing her gently on the lips.

By the end of the movie all three kids had fallen asleep. "They're so precious," Claire whispered, "I know they're going to be happy here."

"It feels so good to know that we are bringing them love and happiness and they are giving us the same," I said, gently picking Matthew up to take him to bed. "I'll be back for Collin in a minute, I don't want you picking him up," I told Claire as I left the room. My mom soon followed carrying Kate.

A few hours ago the other three children, Jasmine, Nicole and Janet arrived. Nicole and Janet warmed up to everyone quickly and were soon playing tag with Kate out in the garden, but it was Jasmine we were concerned about. She barely looked at us when we asked her to come inside and drew her hand back when Claire reached out. "It's okay Jasmine, we're going to take care of you," Claire said, but Jasmine was quiet, her head hung low as she walked into the house.

She was the eldest of the children and showed the most pain, most likely because she remembers a lot of what she'd been through, whereas the others were too young to remember. She seemed thin for her tall frame, and when we led her to the living room to meet everyone else, she kept to herself and didn't speak to anyone. Claire and I had decided not to rush her or force ourselves on her, we'd allow her to get used to her new surroundings and let her come around in her own time. Maybe if she sees how comfortable the other children are she would soon feel the same.

It crushed my heart to see such a young girl hurting so much and feeling so scared. This was her fourth home in three years, and it soon brought back memories of my own childhood. I knew she didn't trust anyone, including us, how could she? Everyone had let her down.

I watched as Claire sat next to her for a while and tried to make small talk, but Jasmine remained silent, her arms folded, avoiding any eye contact with Claire.

My heart lifted when Tilly was the one that made her smile for the first time as she came up and jumped in Jasmine's lap and licked her face. At first, Jasmine tried to resist, but soon a smile broke out across her face as Tilly continued to lick her, and soon Jasmine was giggling and cuddling with Tilly. From across the room I grinned when I saw Claire and Jasmine share a friendly smile and Claire leaning in to pet Tilly with her. It was a heart-warming sight, and when Claire suggested they go outside and play ball with Tilly, I almost shed a tear when I saw Jasmine nod and pick Tilly up to follow Claire outside. It may take some time, but I had a feeling Jasmine would be just fine.

~

On the day of the welcome party Jill arrived bright and early, eager to get to work, and all the kids, including Jasmine, were eager to help. Jasmine had become fond of Jill when she found out Jill's favorite color was pink, apparently it was Jasmine's too, and yesterday Jill surprised her with a pink jacket and a pink teddy bear. The teddy bear has become her constant companion, and I think she's only taken the jacket off when she goes to bed.

Over the past few days the children have embraced us, and I sense they trust us now. Their smiles are genuine, and when I hear them laugh it melts my heart.

Jill stood in front of the French doors that led out to the garden where the party was being held. With her hand resting on the door handle, she rounded up the kids who quickly surrounded her with bright eyes. "Okay kids, today you are going to have the party of a lifetime, are you ready?"

I laughed when they all cheered and clapped their hands.

Jill knelt at the kid's level and took the two youngest in her arms. "We're going to have pizza!"

The kids cheered.

"We're going to have cake!"

The kids cheered again.

"There's going to be a magic show!"

The cheers grew louder, and the kids were now jumping in the air and raising their arms with excitement.

"Wait, there's more," Jill said with a huge grin, "there's going to be a big bouncy house, clowns and a pony!"

Jasmine suddenly squealed, "a pony? I love ponies!"

"You do?" Claire said with a big smile as she joined the excited group.

One by one the kids followed Claire and Jill out to the garden, Abigail and my mom following close behind with snacks and drinks.

"This is incredible, everyone's so happy," Claire's mom said, setting down a tray of snacks. "I love being here with you and Travis every day and spending my time with these wonderful children, thank you for everything."

"Mom, dad did one last good deed while we were saying our goodbyes to him, he's the one that brought us together, and it's him you should thank."

Crews arrived to set up their apparatus for the party while we set up tables and chairs with some of the kids' help, but the youngest ones were more interested in playing with Tilly and Maggie who Jill brought to spend the day.

Sabela and Slater arrived first with a bag full of gifts for the kids, and Scottie suddenly found six new friends to play with. "Look how well they all get along," Slater said, as we all took a seat at one of the tables.

"I have a feeling Scottie's going to be asking to come over here a lot more often," Sabela laughed.

"I think you're right," I said. "He gave me a quick hello and a high-five, and I haven't seen him since, I think he'll sleep well tonight."

Claire glanced around the area where we were sitting, "where are the twins?"

Sabela pointed to the grassy area under the shade tree, "with Caroline and Abigail."

We all looked to where she pointed and saw our moms sitting on a blanket in the shade playing with Joy and Hope.

"They offered to watch them as soon as we arrived, and well, I couldn't pass up some free time," Sabela confessed.

"That's awesome, we'll take turns watching them so that we can all enjoy the party," Claire suggested.

"That's a great idea Claire, thanks, we appreciate it. We tend to miss out on all the fun," Sabela joked.

Ricky arrived at the same time as Logan and Sadie with even more gifts for the kids. Twenty minutes later Sabela's mom Charlotte and her boyfriend Lorenzo arrived with stuffed animals "for everyone under the age of 10," they stated.

"Claire, Travis, you two have a beautiful family. It's what you've always wanted and I'm so happy for you both," Sabela said, as the tremendous party wound down and we all sat around the large table under the moonlight with strings of white lights illuminating the patio area beautifully.

Jill and Ricky were on the grass sitting in a circle with the four oldest kids reading a story via flashlight, while the two youngest rested in mine and Claire's lap, with Slater and Sabela holding the twins.

"It's been an amazing week," Claire said as she took my hand. "We have you to thank for everything, we wouldn't be here if it wasn't for you."

"Well, not everything," Slater said with a hint of sarcasm, "we had nothing to do with that baby you're carrying."

Claire rolled her eyes and cracked a laugh, "true," she said, gently patting her belly. "This little miracle inside of me is something we thought could never happen. Neither Travis nor I can think of anything else we want in life; it's all here, friends, family and lots of love."

Sabela nodded and took Slater's hand. "I know what you mean, Slater and I feel the same way. I look at our beautiful girls and ask myself how we got so lucky, then I think of Scottie and how he came into our lives. There's nothing more we could wish for, we have it all, family is everything."

"It's going to be a special day for both of you when the adoption papers are finalized so you can adopt Scottie, and that should be happening soon," Claire told Sabela with bright eyes.

"I know, and then it'll be time for another party," she giggled. "I'm not sure if the kids will be able to keep up with us," she joked.

"I think you have that backwards," Slater laughed, "look at those kids with Jill and Ricky, they're still wide awake and here we are barely keeping our eyes open." He nudged Sabela's elbow, "we may have to book our late honeymoon sooner so we can escape and get some rest."

"Have you finally decided where you're going?" Claire asked.

Sabela smiled, "we have, but we're going to wait until next year when the twins are older. I for one am not sure if we can wait that long, but I think Slater's right, we may need to go much sooner. I can't remember the last time we've had any alone time."

"So, where are you going?"

"Well, we don't want to be too far away. Mom and Lorenzo will stay at our place with the kids, and there's another thing, we're house hunting, it seems we've outgrown our existing home." She looked down at Hope sleeping peacefully and chuckled, "I wonder how that happened? Anyway, like I said, we don't want to be in some foreign country in case there's an emergency at home, so we've decided to go to Catalina Island, it's only an hour by boat and then an hour home on the freeway."

Claire's eyes glowed, "oh, Catalina is perfect; as they say, it's the island of Romance. Are you going to Avalon?"

"Yes, Avalon has it all - romantic restaurants, sandy beaches, snorkeling and boats." She laughed, "should I go on? It'll be a week of just Slater and I and some romance."

Slater leaned into Sabela and kissed her on the lips, "definitely some romance."

ABOUT THE AUTHOR

Award winning author, Tina Hogan Grant loves to write stories with strong female characters that know what they want and aren't afraid to chase their dreams. She loves to write sexy and sometimes steamy romances with happy ever after endings.

She is living life to the fullest in a small mountain community in Southern California with her husband and two dogs. When she is not writing she is probably riding her ATV, kayaking or hiking with her best friend – her husband of twenty-five years.

www.tinahogangrant.com

facebook.com/Tina.Hogan.Grant.Author

instagram.com/tina_hogan_grant

amazon.com/Hogan-Grant-Tina/e/B07HLDXDGV

bookbub.com/authors/tina-hogan-grant

www.ingramcontent.com/pod-product-compliance
Lightning Source LLC
Chambersburg PA
CBHW031157010826
48971CB00012B/750